ADVANCE PRAISE FOR

DOCTOR ROBERT

"Lopez's deep dive into physician power, nefarious plotting, and counseling's potential for dangerous relationships creates a thoroughly thought-provoking, unexpected scenario readers will find hard to put down as they follow Robbie into the therapist's office and beyond the power of self-examination into dangerous territory.

Highly recommended for its juxtaposition of suspense, coming-of-age experiences, and inviting discourses on life and death, *Doctor Robert* is a winning page-turner that's hard to neatly categorize and equally difficult to put down."

—DIANE DONOVAN FOR THE MIDWEST BOOK REVIEW

"*Doctor Robert* by Bobby Lopez is a masterfully written novel that plunges readers into the heart of a young boy's struggle against family discord and personal loss. Lopez delivers a deep narrative that transcends the typical boundaries of a psychological thriller . . . Robbie, the protagonist, is portrayed with incredible depth. Lopez masterfully constructs a vivid psychological environment, making Robbie's fears and victories emotionally authentic.

The storytelling is exquisite, with Bobby Lopez's prose flowing seamlessly from chapter to chapter, weaving complex emotional threads into a tapestry that captures the imagination and sympathy. The dialogue especially engages with philosophical insights that provide each character's perspectives and wisdom . . .

The book is a must read for adult readers who enjoy thought-provoking literature, medical thrillers, or fiction that explores the mind. It is worthy of more than five stars."

—5-STAR READERS' FAVORITE REVIEW

"Lopez explores the themes of losing a maternal figure, fitting in, and the search for genuine connections . . . The book further delves into the struggles of socializing and the anxiety that often accompanies it. Ultimately, the author emphasizes the importance of genuine connections, where people truly care for and support one another. Recommended."

—AMANDA HANSON FOR THE US REVIEW OF BOOKS

DOCTOR ROBERT

BY BOBBY LOPEZ

Doctor Robert

Doctor Robert will demand,
Doctor Robert will command,
With a helping hand you won't understand.

If you're around,
He'll knock you down.
If you give him a call,
He won't be there at all.

He's a man who will mislead,
He'll make you recede and accede,
But no one can supersede
Like Doctor Robert.

Doctor Robert will prefer,
Doctor Robert will concur,
That he acts more like an entrepreneur.

If you're feeling lost,
His sessions come at high cost.
If you consume his special pill,
You will still lose your will.

He's a man with great greed,
He preys upon those in need,
But no one can succeed
Like Doctor Robert.

Doctor Robert will lie,
Doctor Robert will make you die,
Because he won't let you say goodbye.

When you're feeling well,
He'll drag you down to hell.
When the bells ring in your head,
He'll make you wish you were dead.

He's a man who heeds no creeds,
Who leads with many misdeeds,
But no one can supersede,
But no one can succeed,
Like Doctor Robert.

PROLOGUE

IN THE WEE HOURS OF THE NIGHT

In the wee hours of the night, while weary souls were sound asleep, I lay in my bed trying to count sheep. But my counting was ceaselessly interrupted by the intruding thoughts pervading my brain. Endless thoughts of fear and dread floated through my mind, making my eyes tired thinking of it, while simultaneously making me too anxious to sleep. Every night, I lay under the cold covers of life put upon me by fate, depriving me of vital slumber that would make anyone curl up and cry.

A decade's worth of memories bore down on me. Its heaviness seemed far beyond what my small shoulders could carry. I was little more than a child, but I was an old soul trapped in a young body. I lay in my small, dimly lit bedroom while the moonlight cast eerie shadows on the walls, amplifying the weight of my thoughts and fears. Darkness surrounded me like a cloak of shadows. I was unable to gather the power to shut my eyes, and tune out the deafening white noise of my life, or tune out the reverberating voices of my mom and dad shouting over each other in the rooms nearby. Every night the shouting sustained itself for hours, the intensity seemingly escalating with each passing night. Yet I didn't know what would warrant such shouting. The noise from their quarrels just seemed to increase each night as I tried to sleep.

But I didn't always hear their noisy clamor at night, I used to sleep in serene silence. The silence was always upheld by unbreakable unity. Regardless of our individual pursuits, we still made time to be together. When I tossed bread to ducks in a park, my mom and dad were constantly guiding me on the proper way to feed them. In the small pond we visited, the ducks often swam in groups of three. Whether it was rain or shine, they could still swim powerfully across the pond, united in their activity. While feeding the ducks wasn't a preferred pastime, spending time with my family brought me joy. And my mom would gently say, "Someone has to feed them, Robbie. Imagine how hungry they are in the cold. Even though they are getting by, they won't be able to maintain that strength forever. Someone has to come by and help empower them when they're down."

My mom always seemed to know what to say, and when I struggled to grasp words, she was there to help me expand my vocabulary. I became a very proficient reader due to her influence. She was willing to spend hours upon hours every night, teaching me how to read efficiently and accurately. The dictionary became a daily friend of mine, as my mom would have a word of the day for me to learn, and I would recite the definition and write it in sentences until I produced a satisfactory understanding of its definition and syntax. One time I was struggling with the word "polymath." I just couldn't get the definition to stick in my head, even after using it in sentences. Because the definition of polymath wasn't simply being a genius; it meant that you had wide-ranging knowledge in many areas. At the time that nuance was hard for me to grasp, and when my mom would occasionally quiz me on previous words, polymath was the most repeated question. After yet another failed attempt at memorizing it, my mom came up with a genius way for me to learn it. She taught me about Latin roots, because over 60 percent of the English language contains Latin or Greek roots. Much of the English language also derives from Germanic and Romance languages (mainly Spanish, Italian, and French), so-called because they derived from Latin, the language used in ancient Rome. After I learned this, I began memorizing Latin and Greek roots, as well as new vocabulary. Then I learned that *poly* means "many," and *math* refers to the process of learning. Subsequently, I barely had any troubles with words because I could just refer to the root, or just normally memorize it.

When I would tell stories like this to my classmates, they ridiculed me and said things such as "Why would you do that?" Sometimes they couldn't understand what I was saying and asked me to rephrase and not use such "big words." But I was not ashamed to utilize sophisticated language. To give an example, it's been said that literature tells extraordinary stories with ordinary words. So imagine what stories can be told when we use extraordinary words. My speech can reach and teach those who don't wish to beseech. Yet they just couldn't grasp how important it was to be consummate. They'd rather mimic the language of those around them, lacking comprehension or perception, lacking the power to learn. The English language contains hundreds of thousands of words, and an advanced understanding of it allowed me to communicate more effectively with more nuances. So if someone has trouble understanding what I say, they can gain a basic understanding of Latin roots to help glean the meaning, or gather it from context. And if you don't know that, there's always the dictionary, and there's nothing wrong with that.

In contrast, my dad was single-handedly responsible for my unparalleled physical prowess for my age. Our house boasted exercise equipment, and he made it my daily ritual to exercise before I could do any other activity. I began to increase my skill at an astonishing rate, and was lifting a plate on each side of the bar for bench press alone. My dad resembled an army drill sergeant, urging me to push beyond my limits. Yet he was always ready to spot me when I worked out, always there to help me improve. But it was the help I required to perfect myself. When I was benching and I struggled to push the bar all the way, my dad would barely lift it with his fingers so I would move most of the weight, and sometimes he yelled out aphorisms to encourage me. My dad didn't handhold me; if I needed him, he was there, but he expected me to do some of the work on my own. I didn't need a father who spoke banal platitudes such as "You can be whoever you want." I needed a father who taught me values such as determination and the importance of fitness, and I wouldn't have it any other way.

Sometimes kids my age would compliment my physical prowess, yet more often they would chastise and preach to me the concept of humility. Unfortunately for them, modesty was not in my long list of vocabulary. My achievements were not boastful, but a reflection of reality. And those who criticized me often did so out of envy, their primal instincts clouding their judgment. I learned not to be swayed by the opinions of others, recognizing that dislike often stemmed from baseless reasons. I refused to partake into such inanity. Nor did I want to waste my nights pondering the reasons for their disdain. That wasn't how I wanted to exercise my life.

Reflecting on these memories prompted me to ponder my age. Despite being just ten years old, my demeanor and intellect set me apart from my peers. Classmates, parents, and teachers often remarked on my apparent maturity. The reasons behind this perception remained elusive, perhaps attributed to my physical appearance. When I would look into a mirror, I confronted the stark contrast between my external visage and my inner self. My sculpted muscles revealed countless hours of rigorous training. My piercing blue eyes, like sapphires shining in sunlight, hinted at a hidden allure that belied the surface. Towering above others, I exuded a quiet demeanor that contrasted with my height and muscular appearance. My dark, lustrous hair served as a veil shrouding the complexities of my thoughts and the shadows of untold stories that lingered within. I didn't look like a polymath, and the world around me seemed to agree with me. The inherent contradiction between my outward appearance and inner depth alienated my peers. Others couldn't, or wouldn't, connect with me. But I refused to mimic the world to connect with them. And because of this, I didn't really possess any friends. I was cursed with intelligence. But despite the lack of connection, I could always rely on my relationship with my parents and the activities we would do to foster happiness.

These daily routines exhausted me so much that I would sleep like a baby, forcing my mom to rouse me as I was sleeping far past the single digits. Memories like these would remind me of the unity of my family, and these memories made their absence more painful. But now those memories, once within reach, now seemed distant. Some insidious force was causing a ripple in my family, and producing a piercing noise that prevented me from sleeping. In these quiet moments, I pondered the fleeting nature of happiness, along with the fragility of life. With the weight of the world on my shoulders, I carried burdens no child should bear. And I grappled with hardships that were far beyond my years.

As I continued my struggle to sleep, the deafening noise seeped into my very soul and brought tears to my eyes. I cried so hard just to make the pain end; maybe then I could finally sleep. But after crying for what seemed an eternity, the sound of shouting from the other room stopped, and I heard hushed footsteps coming closer.

The door creaked open, and my mom entered, her presence a soothing light in the darkness. She wore a white gown, which contrasted greatly with the somber atmosphere. She settled herself on the edge of my bed.

"Robbie, what's wrong?"

After hastily wiping the tears from my eyes, I managed to tell her, "Nothing is wrong."

But she smiled softly and murmured, "Robbie, you've never been good at lying, and I could hear you crying. Just tell me how you feel."

"It's just the endless shouting, day in, day out. It never stops. It's ceaseless. Why can't you just stop fighting with Dad? What could possibly warrant such arguments every night?"

She turned and looked at the door, as if searching for answers in the emptiness beyond. Then her eyes met mine once more and she gazed down, a mix of pain and determination etched on her face. She looked at me again, then once again looked down. She began to speak, but the words faltered and she stopped herself. She attempted this again and again until she began to cry. I watched the tears slowly drip down her face until she was finally able to express what she wanted to say.

"Robbie, when I was younger, I felt ashamed about my body, about who I was. Like you, I loved to exercise and make sure my body was in perfect shape. It didn't matter how I did it, whether I starved myself, or exercised hours upon hours a day to hit every muscle. I wanted perfection, but it wasn't enough for me. So I received breast implants to make my body look even better. And for a time, it did give me happiness from the way I looked and the way people looked at me. But the chemicals in the silicone infected my right breast and affected its cell growth. I was diagnosed with breast cancer. I had a mastectomy, the most painful experience of my life, and I thought that was the end of it. I met your father and immediately fell in love with him, as he didn't care about my imperfection or my surgically removed body part. Then I had you, my little angel, my greatest gift to the world.

"As the years passed and I tucked my baby boy in at night, I thought I was cancer free. But the cancer spread undetected from my breast to the rest of my body, and a tumor formed in my heart. This happened right after your fourth birthday. The doctors said the likelihood of survival was nearly none, and I would die within a year. But I didn't want to give up on my boy. I wanted you to grow up with a loving mother by your side. I wanted to kiss you goodnight as much as I could. So I did everything I could to keep myself alive as long as possible. I wanted your childhood to be perfect. I went to monthly radiation appointments, and felt the radiation give me continual fatigue. I received constant chemotherapy, lost all of my hair, and was forced to wear a wig. I consumed various types of medications to fight the cancer, and I gained weight and lost that perfect body I felt so attached to. And everyone around me told me I was nuts; they kept incessantly telling me that I was fighting a losing battle, and I should just make peace with what was going to happen. Your father, I love him, but he thinks I'm pushing myself too hard. He thinks I'm giving myself unnecessary pain and trauma.

"And I do have a lot of pain, Robbie; it hurts so much every day. I fight that pain. I've been fighting for nearly six years now. But none of that matters to me. All that mattered was for you to grow up loving yourself more than I ever could. All I ever wanted was for you to have the best childhood possible. I just wanted you to sleep soundly at night and not worry about problems that no child should ever be forced to think about."

As she said all of this to me, I couldn't help but let out every fragment of sadness I had. What hurt the most was that I remember attending her doctor visits with her, and I noticed her losing her hair, and gaining weight. But I just thought that's how she was; I didn't think to ask why. I was such an idiot, and it made me so sad. Despite the wisdom beyond my years, I still wasn't smart enough to realize what was happening.

While I looked at her, my body was trembling and the tears just kept on streaming from my eyes. I never shed so many tears before. I let everything out—every fragment of sadness and despair. All I had or ever had in emotions, I released at that moment.

A few minutes passed and I kept bawling, but I was able to pay attention to my mom's next few words. "What I'm trying to say, Robbie, is that I'm not gonna be around much longer. I'm gonna die, and I can't fight it much more. But now it's your time to fight, Robbie. It's not fair that I can't be your mother anymore, but it's just a part of life. Sometimes life is unfair and takes away something you love. It means you're going to have challenges growing up that other kids won't have. And it pains me that I won't be able to help you with them. But it doesn't mean something is wrong with you; it's just what makes you who you are. And I know you can fight those problems, I know you can fight the grief of losing me, because you're like me. I know wherever you'll go in life, you'll continue to fight."

"I don't want to, Mom. I don't want to go on in life knowing that you won't be there by my side."

"You're gonna have to, Robbie. I know it's not fair, believe me, I know. But the true fighters fight even when it's not fair, when everything is stacked against you. Even if you think you'll lose, you fight anyway. It's not something everybody has, but I know you have it."

As she said this, a swirling storm of emotions collided within me, creating a tempest that engulfed my thoughts. I turned away and lay with my back towards her. Her shoulders slumped and her hand trembled as she brushed away a tear. She kissed me on my side, walked out of my room, and closed the door to let me try and sleep.

But now the white noise was at its apex. The noise was so boisterous that I couldn't concentrate on counting sheep. My mind kept wandering to everything I would face in the future. And as I continued to weep, I couldn't bring myself to sleep.

PART 1:
DE PROFUNDIS

TEARS FROM HEAVEN

"Wake up, Robbie."

Slowly my eyes adjusted to the faint light, and I realized I was lying face down on my bed. I turned my body, shifting from darkness to the pale glow of the room. I was engulfed in a suffocating shroud of blackness. My room was painted plain white and contained no decorations on the walls. Yet the feeble rays of the light bulbs barely illuminated the space, unable to fully penetrate the oppressive gloom. I found myself caught between the lingering tendrils of a bad dream and the weight of reality.

The dream, a haunting replay of a night from two years earlier, had become a recurring nightmare. It clung to my mind, refusing to loosen its grip. It's odd that I dreamed of a memory, and in perfect detail. I longed for other types of dreams, like living in a chocolate factory, or exploring a treasure island. Yet the past had a tenacious grip on my subconscious, an inescapable reminder of what was.

"Come on, Robbie, wake up."

My dad's voice broke through the fog of my thoughts. His usual disheveled self was familiar, but today there was an undeniable sadness etched on his face. Since my mom's cancer had worsened, he usually paid no attention to his appearance. His shoulders slumped, burdened by some sort of weight. His eyes, with prominent bags, were on the verge of bloodshot. Seeing my usually strong and unwavering father in such a state was jarring. It was June, and with sixth grade behind me, I hoped for a carefree summer and uninterrupted nights of peaceful slumber. I hoped night after night.

But something in his voice told me that this moment was different. I rose from my bed, sat down, and watched my dad struggle to find the right words. A sorrow permeated the room as he finally managed to find the right words. The words echoed with such sadness and despair that no human being should ever have the responsibility of saying them.

"Mom passed away last night."

An indescribable pain plagued my brain as soon as he said these words. I was rendered speechless. She couldn't be gone. Could she? What would I do without her? How could she be dead? The questions ricocheted through my mind, each one a painful reminder of the void that now loomed ahead, an emptiness I couldn't fathom.

It had been a relentless battle for my mom, her body ravaged by cancer and her spirit weighed down by the burdens it brought. Besides ingesting many medications and increasing her chemotherapy, she started increasingly drinking vodka. She didn't have the power to battle the disease on her own, so she drank alcohol to assist in her battle. But her habit disempowered her even more, as she relied on the drink for any sort of happiness or purpose. Every week, my mom would buy another bottle of vodka, and every week the alcohol within would be gone. At one point I mistakenly took a sip, thinking it was water. It burned like a fire ignited inside my throat, and I immediately spat it out. How my mom could ingest such a substance day after day perplexed me.

It all took a heavy toll on her mind. She soon began to lose control of her body, as the cancer began chipping away at her brain. She would forget a subject in the middle of a conversation, or stumble when walking around the house. It actually came to a point where she started to faint when standing for too long, and hit objects around the house as she fell to the ground. The cancer had hollowed her vibrant presence into an empty shell.

Unable to bear witness to her suffering any longer, my dad made the difficult decision to admit her to a hospital. Life support had become her tether to the world, as her consciousness slipped away. Days turned to weeks, and the doctors eventually delivered the heart-wrenching news that nothing more could be done. They suggested transferring her to some sort of home care for further support. I wasn't involved in all the details, but I fully believed that she could recover. I couldn't fathom that someone so close to me could be removed from my life. Despite the doctors' somber advice, my dad arranged for her to be transported to our home on a stretcher and acquired all the necessary equipment to provide for her needs.

Our living room had become a makeshift hospital. I was desperate to shield her from the restless assault of the disease. The walls echoed with the sounds of medical equipment and heavy breathing, a symphony of beeps and whispered prayers. Each passing day etched lines of exhaustion upon my face, my heart heavy with the weight of watching her slip away. But she continued to fight, her mind clinging to life even though her body remained dormant. But now, even that battle had come to an end.

After the brief shock, my dad left the room, leaving me to wrestle with my emotions. My dad wasn't one to mince words, and he usually carried himself with confidence and power. But he loved my mom, and it seemed as if all the power had been sucked out of him, forcing me to figure out the loss on my own. I walked into the living room and saw a pale corpse on a stretcher. It was surreal, gazing at the remains of someone I loved so deeply. She was lifeless, and hauntingly still. I wished I had the power to restore her, to make her look peaceful once again. But all I could do was stand there, engulfed in a numbness that rendered me motionless.

As people from the morgue gathered around and prepared to move the body, I remained frozen, merely a spectator in my own home. The room was dimly lit, the workers moved with quiet efficiency, a stark contrast to the apathy inside me.

One woman paused, her eyes filled with sympathy, and offered a comforting remark, "Your mom was really brave to last as long as she did. I'm sure she's sprinkling love down on you from heaven."

My hands clenched at my sides. As the worthless words washed over me, my mind raced with the frustration of the superficiality of her comment.

She continued, "The death of a parent is very common, but therapy really helps in times like this. You should consider it."

Each word was like a wave crashing against the walls of my heart. The distance between her and me was like a chasm unable to be bridged. If she really was so caring of my suffering, she wouldn't have asked someone else to care about me instead. Why would someone say that to me? How could someone say that to me? Yet I lacked the power to move my lips, my mind concentrating on the pale corpse in front of me. So she moved on, leaving me to grapple with the loss in solitude.

They carried my mom away, her final departure marked by the closing of a van's door. I retreated to my room, hoping to find solace in the familiar embrace of my bed. I lay down and attempted to rest. But then, my gaze fell upon my dresser to a photograph of my mom and myself—a memory frozen in time. While lying on my bed, I reached and grabbed it. I was in a baby wrap and she was rocking me in her arms. She loved to sing me lullabies that would always put me to sleep. The picture was worn and faded, yet it did nothing to temper the pure joy of the moment. It was bathed in a soft and golden light, casting a warm glow over us. She and I wore dark clothing at that moment, but her happiness radiated despite the darkness. Her serene smile was like a shiny star in the night sky. It held a weight that transcended its physical form, and its presence threatened to overwhelm me.

Anger surged within me when I realized that she would no longer be there to sing me lullabies. I raised the photograph in my hand, my heart conflicted with a whirlwind of emotions. I wanted to slam it down into a myriad of fragments. I desired never to know this feeling of loss again. But I couldn't. The desire to shatter it warred with the worry of erasing her memory. Her presence exerted such a profound effect on my life that I couldn't let go. I wasn't holding a photograph. I was holding onto a piece of her, and I held onto it tightly. Tears from heaven rolled across my cheek, and my body began to shiver in fear. As each second ticked away, the room grew colder as the despair from the picture increased. The picture held power over me, like a siren's song singing me sweet and haunting melodies that fractured my heart. I slowly placed the photograph back on the dresser, lingering with it for many minutes.

As I lay on my bed, the photograph only increased the pain, and my body bore the weight of grief and exhaustion. Like the picture frame that contained its delicate beauty, my body was a fragile vessel that bore recollections and emotions that threatened to burst at the seams. Memories of my mom flooded my mind, each one intensifying the ache within my heart. More memories of my mom and me just kept on rolling through my mind, and I couldn't stop them. The pain just grew greater and greater. I knew at that moment that grief would forever accompany me into the night.

JOHN 14:27

As my scrawny little hands clung to my mom's firm grip, the heavy wooden doors of the church creaked open. Sorrow lingered in the atmosphere, blending with the scent of flesh flowers and faint incense. The sunlight filtered a kaleidoscope of colors through intricate stained glass windows. The echoes of footsteps reverberated off the high ceiling, which amplified the solemnity within the ancient walls. As I stepped inside, my heart pounded and my hands trembled, bracing me for the painful reality that awaited.

Guiding me down an aisle, my mom led us to a pew near the front, and we sat down. The dimly lit building buzzed with voices, creating an eerie but bustling ambience. Candles scattered throughout the room, each flickering flame whispered sadness and remembrance into the hushed air. Faces of sorrow surrounded me as they conversed in hushed tones. Amidst the crowd, images of a man adorned the walls, statues, paintings, and murals. Yet there was no joy in any depiction. Each portrait showed the man's miserable countenance, as if he carried an enduring burden upon his shoulders. Particularly striking was a picture of a woman cradling this man, her demeanor graceful and unaffected, as if she could release him from his burden. Above the altar loomed a colossal cross, the man attached to it, a figure of dejection and lifelessness. The grandeur with which it hung evoked a sense of pride, not misery. But the meaning eluded me.

My mom leaned over and spoke in a hushed whisper, "Now, remember, Robbie, Alexis's parents have just died. Death leaves an everlasting mark upon the person's soul, and it can never heal. It's important to help the family grieve as much as you can. They aren't going to ask for help, nor do they have to, but what matters is that we help anyway. We can't go back to our daily lives and pretend that death never happened. If we really care for her, we have to sacrifice time in our lives to help them move on, otherwise we have no business calling her our friend. It's why I brought you, Robbie. She loves to see you and knows how important you are to me. I know you love her too, it's why you called her Aunt Alexis all your life; you just didn't fully understand it. People who truly love each other never give up on each other. This is the time where Alexis will really see who cares about her, and we're here to show that we're one of those people."

• • •

"Robbie?"

The voice brought me back to the present. I was silent, my gaze fixed on the pew in front of me.

"I was just telling your father that your mother's funeral is all in order for tomorrow. People will start to show up for the viewing in a few minutes."

I remained silent.

"Your mom was a brave woman, and I'm sure she's in a better place."

Again, silence was my only response. After a few moments, Alexis walked away. Though she had generously helped plan and finance the funeral, more than most would do, her words were the only interaction we had shared in the past few weeks. She was a businesswoman now, and couldn't afford to attend the funeral or the viewing. Alexis was moving on to continue her life—lucky her.

After so many years, I found myself in the same place as before, a giant hollow building celebrating something I didn't understand. The difference now was that I had one fewer person to help guide me. My dad lingered somewhere, but all I yearned for was solitude, losing myself in my own thoughts. But I heard voices starting to grow louder.

The first person to approach me was Maddy Phrey, a girl my age. She was clad in an all-black dress, which juxtaposed the bright beauty of her body. Her radiant blonde hair fell around her shoulders, each strand shining with a life of its own. She had hypnotic blue eyes that mirrored an ocean's depth, reflecting the myriad hues of a sunset on a horizon. She was like a star gymnast; her body was poetry in motion, where strength and grace danced in perfect harmony, mirroring the captivating allure of her beauty.

But beyond her beauty, her intelligence eclipsed everything else. Inside a bustling classroom, Maddy Phrey exuded an air of quiet confidence. When our teacher delved the class into interpreting the Bible, Maddy's eyes sparkled with intrigue, her mind already working at a rapid pace.

When we read John 14:27, the teacher asked, "What does God mean by 'Peace I leave with you, peace I give to you. I do not give to you as the world gives. Do not let your hearts be troubled. Do not be afraid'?"

Maddy's hand shot up, eager to express the deeper meaning. But another person threw up their hand, and the teacher called on them.

"God gives us peace."

"Yes. Yes. But can you go a little deeper?" the teacher responded.

And then Maddy was finally called on. With an effortless command of language she explained, "The line refers to Divine Providence, reminding us that we can find peace and love through God even in challenging circumstances. It signifies a deep contentment with God due to His omnipresence in our lives."

Her intelligence was a beacon in the classroom, inspiring me to strive for greater intellectual depth. Yet we possessed a subtle difference in savoir faire. Maddy displayed remarkable intelligence, but she never allowed it to hinder her ability to interact with others and blend in effortlessly.

We attended a prestigious middle school, so all our classmates shared some form of brainpower. This environment seemingly made it easier for Maddy to make friends and avoid being looked down upon. Since I was not as socially adept as she was, we were socially distant. Still, I could not help but notice the meticulous attention to detail that Maddy gave her appearance. It gave me a pang of embarrassment as I glanced down at my wrinkled shirt and untied tie. While my mom shared Maddy's appreciation for aesthetics and always tried to make me look presentable, I simply did not share the same level of concern. Yet this deepened my admiration for Maddy, as she exemplified a perfectionism that I would strive for. I recognized that it wasn't love, but rather a longing for an opportunity to become friends, or perhaps more than friends.

If I desired, I could have worked up the courage to converse with her. Courage wasn't the issue. The complexities of social interaction were the problem. How would I initiate a conversation? What topics should be broached and for how long? It wasn't enough to maintain a logical dialogue; one must also infuse it with charm. How do I subtly slide the conversation to gain her affection? Should I be direct about asking her out or become friends first? But since I could not be friends with Maddy without approaching her, what then?

After careful deliberation, I realized that answers to these questions varied between individuals. Yet striking the perfect balance between all these elements seemed insurmountable. Trying to methodically control a conversation was nearly impossible, and the common response was to just "act natural." But this raised more questions. Could I even act natural when I lacked a solid foundation in socializing? Were there implicit conversational rules that I risked breaking? How could one define "acting natural"? The answers eluded me, leaving me frustrated whenever I contemplated having a conversation with Maddy.

I eventually accepted the fact that engaging with others was a lost cause, but this only heightened my infatuation and the agony of being unable to act upon my desires. Consequently, I rarely uttered a word to Maddy. Her approach during the viewing was one of the few occasions she initiated a conversation with me. I could see her approaching from the corner of my eye. Amidst these swirling thoughts, I realized that for the first time, I had to summon the power to engage in a conversation with Maddy.

Maddy drew closer, her mother by her side, and they took a seat next to me on the pew. Their presence was a slight beacon of solace in a sea of mourners. Maddy gently slipped her hand into mine, offering silent support. Her touch provided a brief respite from the immense sadness that threatened to overwhelm me. Gathering a semblance of strength, I redirected my focus to them. They both shared a sad visage, and I could tell they possessed great pity for me.

Maddy spoke first. "Robbie . . . . I'm sure your mother was a brave woman who is in a better place."

Out of all the things she could have said, out of all the things I wanted her to say to me, she chose to echo the same sentiments I kept on hearing. How could she possibly know if my mom had found a better place? How was that supposed to help me? Why resort to platitudes that only served to exacerbate my pain? In that moment, my infatuation dissipated. I instinctively pulled my hand away, turning my gaze to the man on the cross above us.

Maddy's disappointment was palpable as she looked down, her mother quickly recognizing the need to intervene.

"Your mother is with God now, Robbie. God is looking after your mother and she is sending you down love from heaven. I know she is so proud of you, and proud of how strong you're handling this. With your mother's passing, God teaches us Divine Providence. God shows us love in many ways, all throughout the day. But even in hard times, when God's love doesn't seem visible, God's love is still there. Even in acts that can seem terrible, goodness can still come from it. I'm sure that God . . ."

I tuned out from Mother Teresa's sermon, and stared at the cross. Her words intertwined with the frustration rising within me. While she was still imposing her lecture, out of the corner of my eye I could see Maddy's mother wearing a necklace with a cross. From her flaunting jewelry and overlong monologue, it was easy to decipher that she was religious. She knew every in and out of life, because of a bestselling book that boasted such knowledge of how the world was created in seven days. The kind of person who couldn't tie a shoe without consulting what it meant for her relationship with god. Too bad her god couldn't decipher my desires, and help me carry the weight of my anguish. I questioned how her unwavering faith could provide solace in my darkest hour.

". . . But this wasn't fully developed until St. Thomas Aquinas and his Summa Theologica . . ."

She was still talking? How the hell did she start talking about this? But finally after god knows how long, Maddy nudged her on the shoulder, and looked at her mother disapprovingly. Her mother sighed, and they got up from the pew and prepared to walk away.

But Maddy looked at me keenly and kindly, and said to me, "Robbie, maybe we could hang out this summer?"

I lacked the power to respond. The weight of it all hung heavy on my shoulders, rendering me speechless and detached from the world around me. So I just remained in silence until Maddy, in sadness, walked away slowly.

It was then that Lauro Ricketts, Maddy's best friend, approached me. Lauro's long dark hair flowed freely, a stark and striking indication of his powerful spirit. His towering figure exuded strength and stability, a clear contrast to my own fragile state. Lauro looked like an ancient oak in a field of saplings, a testament to the strength that seemed to emanate from his figure. He hugged Maddy for a few seconds, then walked towards me. He stood looking at me near the pew, then slowly sat next to me. His presence was a silent acknowledgment of the pain I carried.

Lauro sat in silence for a few minutes. Empathy was in his eyes, even if it was misplaced. I could tell he was pondering the words to use, but he finally grasped a sentence in a voice with genuine concern.

"Robbie, I just want you to know that I know how you feel. I lost my grandpa, and to me, he was amazing. But I bet your mom is meeting him right now and they are happy together wherever they are. I know what you're going through. Just know that I'm here for you and I truly understand how you feel."

No, you don't. Nobody knew what I was going through. How could he possibly understand the depths of my pain? The loss of a mother, and the void it created, was something that no one could truly comprehend unless they had experienced it themselves. His attempt to comfort me with empty words rubbed salt on a fresh wound. The ache in my heart grew even stronger as I yearned for someone who could truly understand the magnitude of my grief, someone who wouldn't attempt to diminish it with hollow condolences.

I clenched my fists and avoided making eye contact with Lauro. Every word he spoke felt like a sharp knife, reopening the wound of my loss. My mind was a whirlwind of anger and frustration, questioning how anyone could truly understand the pain of losing a mother. My silence conveyed the depth of my emotions, as I struggled to find the power to respond.

After I didn't respond, he ultimately stood up and left the pew. But before leaving, he stopped for a moment and turned at me to say, "I want you to know, I'll always be here for you."

As Lauro attempted to console me, memories of my mother flooded my mind. I could almost feel her warm embrace, hear her comforting voice, and see her gentle smile. The realization that I would never experience those moments again intensified the ache in my heart. The void left by her absence was overwhelming, and the meaningless words offered by others only served as a painful reminder of what I had lost.

It was bemusing. I barely knew Lauro, and he tried to bridge the gap between us as if we were lifelong friends. His attempts to grasp for words meant nothing to me, leaving me feeling powerless amidst the overwhelming grief that consumed me.

But that was the running theme of the day. The hours stretched on, and one by one people from all walks of life approached my pew, each offering their own brand of hollow comfort. Classmates, teachers, and unfamiliar family members stepped forward, their toothless mouths moving in a rehearsed rhythm, as if reciting lines from a therapeutic self-help manual. Whether it was "She's in a better place," "I know what you're going through," or "I'll always be here for you," they all gave variations of worthless words. Many of them stumbled over their phrases as they uttered them, like actors unable to remember their lines. It was as if they were handed a script, but failed to internalize their meaning. And yet these meaningless phrases were meant to be my only consolation in this time of grief.

As each person passed by, they amplified my profound sense of emptiness. Their words echoed in the hollowness of the chapel, adding to the immense silence that enveloped me. I yearned for someone to truly understand the depth of my pain, to hold me and acknowledge the void left by my mother's absence. Besides my dad, I didn't have a family. I didn't have anyone who could truly comfort me. It felt as though I was drowning in an endless abyss, desperately reaching out for a lifeline. But I was met only with empty platitudes that did little to bridge the gap between my heartache and their understanding. I knew they would forget all about this moment as soon as they left, but I would remember it for eternity. And the only thing I'd have were empty words that couldn't hope to fill the void.

As the viewing drew to a close, my eyes were drawn to the imposing figure of a man on the cross above the altar. I knew his name, but he was ultimately just another man. As the empty words continued to echo around me, I couldn't help but question him. His outstretched arms seemed to reach out to me, as if expecting me to find solace in his presence and the presence of others. The man, who was supposed to provide solace and answers, felt distant and detached. The promises of divine love and providence seemed hollow, unable to offer the tangible comfort I craved. In these dark moments, I questioned whether this man truly cared about my pain. He seemed to be looking down on me, as if he was expecting something from me, to be empowered in his presence and the presence of others. How could the distant figure, who had suffered his own pain, understand the depths of my grief? And I could just hear the words coming out of his mouth: "I do not give to you as the world gives." But the meaning eluded me.

3.

BIG WHEELS

I was thinking it over. I couldn't stop thinking. But I couldn't seem to think hard enough. Relentless and unyielding thoughts raced through my mind. I'd been attempting to summon even the faintest memories of my mom. I strained my mind, searching for the image of her face or the sound of her laughter, but it was all a haze. I desperately tried to recall memories of her, but they seemed to breeze by like the wind. It frustrated me to no end. I should have been able to remember her, but I couldn't. I could only remember remembering her. How could someone so significant vanish from my thoughts? How could a person who left such a lasting echo depart from my life? Why was I stuck in the wee small hours of the night?

My teacher walked up to my desk. "Robbie, wake up. Now is the time to listen, not to sleep."

"I couldn't . . . wasn't sleeping. You see, Ms. Blackwell, I close my eyes when I'm thinking about the important issues this class brings up."

I met her gaze, attempting to convey sincerity, but she was unimpressed.

"And what are your thoughts then?"

All the world's problems aren't going to be solved by whining about it in a classroom.

"Uhh . . . Umm . . ."

"That's what I thought. Detention, young man, for sleeping in class."

I wanted to argue, but I lacked the power to pursue this exchange further. Ms. Blackwell's dark skin contrasted with her unconventional hair colors, such as green or purple, just to prove she was behind the wheel of her life. And she didn't tolerate other drivers in her lane. She put me at the front of the row, keenly aware of my disinterest in the class. But I couldn't find any peace, whether it was that classroom or any other. She occasionally tried to coax some interactions out of me, urging me to focus on the class's topics instead of my own musings. It was a religion class, a required "morality" class. The classroom itself was adorned with political propaganda, creating a visual cacophony that clashed with students' subdued expressions. All the students slouched in their seats, their eyes glazed with disinterest. The clock on the wall ticked away the minutes, each one seemingly stretching into eternity in the stifling classroom atmosphere. I was in high school now, just a callow and unseasoned freshman, and it seemed that the classroom walls were closing in on me.

Ms. Blackwell announced, "Now class, I know that there have been a few . . . suicides . . . in your school. I'm concerned that no one has any opportunity to voice their feelings about it."

Her first statement was true. A few suicides had occurred in the school. But I didn't really know the students. When I heard about their deaths, it was no different than reading an article in a newsfeed about students killing themselves. Death became so omnipresent in my world that it didn't make a difference to me. But for the rest of my classmates, it became a topic of gossip and speculation, a game of guessing which mental illnesses they suffered from. At least, that's what I'd gathered from overheard conversations.

She continued, "So I want to give you all that opportunity now. Tell me, what are your thoughts on suicide?"

Maddy Phrey eagerly raised her hand. She always had an opinion ready, aligning perfectly with the class's ideology.

"Thank you, Maddy, but I want an answer from someone else besides you today."

Nobody answered. Silence surrounded the room. I glanced around, noticing my classmates avoiding eye contact, unwilling to participate.

Ms. Blackwell waited and waited, and after what felt like an eternity in silence, the teacher asserted, "You all don't have to talk about it, but I do, and I want to say that . . ."

My interest waned, and I lost track of her words. I wasn't being told how to think, I was being told what to think.

As soon as the bell rang, I hastily packed my backpack and attempted to get out of that class as soon as I could, but my classmates beat me to it. In the hallway, Maddy Phrey walked ahead of me. I planned to find a quiet spot to reflect, when a nameless girl sped past me and Maddy. The girl barely touched me, but brushed Maddy and made her drop her belongings, which scattered before her eyes. I noticed the distress on her face when she got on her knees and attempted to pick up her strewn papers. Somehow I managed to gather enough strength to strike a conversation with Maddy, and help her with the binder she mishandled.

"Here, Maddy, let me help you." My voice was softer than usual.

"Oh, thank you, Robbie."

As I helped Maddy gather her scattered papers, a warmth filled me. It was a small act of kindness, but it brought me a sense of fulfillment. She smiled, her eyes shining with gratitude.

"Maddy, what is this? Did Ms. Perfect actually drop something? To think you could make such a silly mistake! I know you love perfection, so don't let this go to your head!"

"Oh wow, you actually can formulate words. I thought darkly brooding in a corner was more your style?"

We shared a moment of laughter. Pretty soon, I got Maddy's life back in order and all the documents back in her binder. Only one item remained—a poetry book entitled *Lady Lazarus*. I picked it up, a sly remark escaping my lips as I handed it to her.

"A Sylvia Plath fan? I didn't think there were many of those left."

"You know Sylvia Plath? Do you like her poems?" Maddy asked, moving a bit closer to me.

I found them very relatable as I thought of killing myself often.

"I find them very inspirational to have such gruesome subject matter being written by a woman! It represents diversity in our society! I mean, it's really inspirational to everyone everywhere, but especially women. Can't forget them!"

"Oh ha-ha. I'm being serious. Do you like her poetry?" Maddy asked.

"Very much." I gave her a smile. "Her words evoke brutal honesty and raw emotions, not seen that much anymore."

"Yes. Her word choices, her imagery, her . . . her . . . her . . . ."

"Enjambment, occasional rhymes, and much more. Yes, it all lights a spark in a disheartened soul."

Pleasantly surprised by our shared perspective, Maddy voiced a request I should have asked long before. "Maybe we can both discuss more about Ms. Lazarus together sometime?"

"I'd like that."

When I was just about to walk away, she stepped in front of me.

"How about now? You usually sit by yourself and stare into the clouds at lunch. It would be nice to have some company besides Lauro."

"But I thought you were one of the 'cool kids.' Don't you sit by them at lunch?"

"Not at this lunch; they're not here. I usually just sit with Lauro. . . . Speaking of which, here he comes now."

Lauro appeared by my side, nonchalantly slinging his arm around my shoulder.

"Hey champ, sorry about that detention, but don't worry, I doze off in that class all the time. . . ."

Maddy interrupted. "Lauro, I wish you wouldn't. It's important to stay educated."

"I wouldn't call that class education."

He immediately let out a hearty laugh. His laughter was so moving that I had to laugh as well.

After a few seconds, Maddy made another comment. "Well, Lauro, we're adding a third party to our lunch squad. Mr. Shelby here will be joining us."

"That's good. Robbie will actually have some company at lunch now. But I don't know, Maddy, I don't think he could keep up a conversation."

I responded, "Well, Lauro, I usually stay silent around you because I find nothing really likable about you to compliment."

"Ouch. Okay, you convinced me. Maddy gave you some confidence for once, what do you know?"

Looking at Maddy, he stated, "Now don't you two start making out when I'm not looking!"

Maddy smiled and kissed Lauro. As they kissed passionately, a twinge of jealousy raced through me. It stung to see their intimacy, and I felt a silent ache for the affection they shared. In that brief moment, I wondered if I could have been the one kissing her, but the opportunity slipped through my fingers. Perhaps if I had more power, the key to unlocking new pathways in my life would be within my grasp. But I quickly pushed the feeling aside because I didn't desire to dwell on my desires.

It was actually quite brazen to watch as they kissed each other in full force, interlocking their tongues in plain view. I was about to do a sarcastic "cough, cough," but Lauro realized his audience and eventually stopped and pulled away from Maddy's lips. Maddy didn't pull away as fast, but eventually did so. And we all walked away together to the cafeteria, with Lauro holding Maddy's hand.

All three of us sat at a half-empty lunch table, with Maddy and Lauro across from me. Besides us three, no one sat near us, though it didn't stop the typical clamor that surrounded us. The lunchroom buzzed like a melting pot of cliques and social hierarchies, with students huddled together in their groups. It was a chaotic battleground of bombastic blathering and a continual hum of activity that swirled around like a whirlwind. The noise resembled a regimen of the shackles of prisoners walking in unison in a chain gang; it was just routine. I myself always wished for a quieter place, somewhere I could escape the cacophony and truly connect with others.

I struggled to concentrate on the conversation. The constant chatter and clatter was suffocating, drowning out my thoughts. It felt like I had to shout just to vocalize my thoughts.

But Lauro started the conversation. "So Robbie, what do you do in your free time? Or do you ponder your thoughts at home as well?"

I did think, whether in reminiscence or contemplation of the future. I read books, watched movies, or played video games, anything that got me testing my mind. But I had a better answer for him.

"Yes, lots of thinking. Something you obviously don't do very often."

"Ho, ho. We have a real comedian here. I never knew you had such witty comebacks."

I smirked at Lauro's playful jab and replied with sarcasm, "You never knew I had it in me, did you? Well, I never knew you had it in you either."

He chuckled. I decided to change the subject. "Aren't you a receiver for the football team? How's the team going?"

He shrugged. "We haven't won a game."

"You're okay with that?"

"Yeah, no need to be perfect. I don't really care that much. Winning isn't everything, right?"

I found his lack of perfectionism irksome, and I wanted to criticize him. But Maddy, who had been on her phone the whole time, quickly butted in.

"Well, Lauro, tell Robbie your real passion."

"What's that, Maddy?"

She raised her eyebrows gleefully. "Don't you know? Partying."

"Oh Maddy, I know you like to party too."

She smiled. "You're right."

At that point they kept on conversing about things to which I could not relate, nor did I have any interest in.

"Hey Lauro, did you see Jeffrey's comment on my Instagram post? Where he said I should post bikini pics more often because he likes seeing my breasts? That's so sexist—you don't tell a lady that on an Instagram post!"

"Well, that was my first thought too."

Maddy sighed, frustration evident in her voice, "Lauro . . ."

"Ignore him. I saw that you deleted the comment, so let it be. He's just some crackpot with no friends, nobody likes him. If he does it again, I'll have a word with him. He just needs many years of therapy. . . . But speaking about nutcases, you know Charlotte, that theater girl?"

"The one with the crush on you?"

"That one. She still has delusions that I love her secretly. She went up to me in the hall yesterday, telling me how much she loved me, and I quickly declared that I don't like her, at all, and how she should get a psychiatrist to fix what she calls charisma. It actually made her cry."

"Wait, how is it that you can say that to Charlotte, but can't say anything to Jeffrey?"

"Cuz Jeffrey's probably more of a crybaby than Charlotte. Besides, you want that psycho eyeing you and me up for revenge?"

"Good point."

Their laughter filled the air as they delved into gossip about our classmates, their judgments flowing freely, as if they were in a position to judge other people's sanity. I couldn't help but be an outsider on the outskirts of the conversation. They continued to exchange words, but I struggled to find something meaningful to contribute. I was an observer, watching from a distance, unable to fully engage.

As they discussed the madness of others, I couldn't help but wonder what they would think if I opened up about my own struggles. Would they distance themselves from me, afraid of the "mentally ill"? It was a risk I wasn't ready to take. Despite the company, I was a third wheel, hiding my true self behind a mask of normalcy.

• • •

After I made it through a long day of constant lectures, my dad pulled up in his dark truck to pick me up. I trudged inside, and we drove off in silence before my dad attempted to break the ice.

"So was it just another okay day of school?"

"You guessed it."

"Nothing exciting happened?"

"No, not really."

There was nothing interesting to share, and silence filled the space between us. We didn't have anything in common and didn't have anything to talk about day after day.

"Well, I need to tell you something, Robbie. I lost my job."

I could sense the weight of frustration and disappointment in his voice.

"How come?" I asked, trying to show my support.

My dad sighed deeply before launching into the story of what happened, his words filled with a mix of bitterness and resignation.

"I was at the construction site today, building the new government-funded housing project. You know that fifteen-acre field I took you to one time? I was there with my coworkers, building the interior wall on the third floor when our client arrived. She was even more of a bumbling idiot today than usual. She was constantly at the construction site—she loved to crack the whip on my boss. I didn't really talk with her too much, but I overheard many conversations where she complained of her employers cracking down on implementing diversity and equity in everything she handled. They must have cracked the whip harder on her more than us, as she said the word diversity more than any other word in the English language. And this would echo in what she came to say next. Her employers changed the architectural plans at the last minute because there were concerns of no unisex bathrooms next to the traditional bathroom clusters. We couldn't alter or add another bathroom next to it because it would interfere with our previous layout. Our boss tried to reason with her, suggesting we could add the bathrooms somewhere else on the floor. But then she went into a tantrum and started yelling about how that would make people feel 'discriminated,' or 'minoritized,' or . . . I don't know. It was along the lines of them having very sensitive feelings, and the feeling of being discriminated mattered more than if you were actually discriminated. But implementing that change meant redoing everything we had already built, using up materials and time, costing the company thousands. That would take us weeks, putting us over deadlines. And ridiculously, even if there was a change in the ticket, the company couldn't charge extra. This infuriated my boss and put all my coworkers on edge. But not my problem anymore. I'm glad I don't have to deal with her anymore. Privileged people like that don't respect the people who set the wheels in motion.

"But that's not even the best part. She sent everyone in a spiral. Demoing that massive building would require hours of back-breaking work with sledgehammers and jackhammers. And there's this guy, Pac-Man, well, his real name is Packer, but I like to get under his skin by calling him Pac-Man. Because he's the laziest and fattest sack of shit I've ever met. I rarely saw him working around us. It's like he always wanders off getting tools or going to the bathroom. At first I didn't realize why management didn't fire him. But then I overheard the foreman complaining to the owner who visited one day. The owner explained that it would look bad if they fired Packer, as Packer was Black. Because then he could hire the NAACP to sue the company, which would force the company to pay thousands of dollars in reparations, and tarnish the company's reputation. I overheard Packer saying a few times where he threatened to sue his previous employers if they fired him. And the threats always worked, as no matter how big the company was, the company was more afraid of his race. Packer simply used the tools at his disposal to beat the system. So me and my coworkers were stuck with him. People like him like to use their race to get ahead in life. And it works, because people don't know how to talk about race, so they find ways of avoiding the topic.

"But anyways, Packer was complaining about all the hard work ahead. 'Guys, we're gonna be out here the rest of the day using the sledge-hammers.' So I decided to butt in. 'Why do you care, Pac-Man? We all know that you're not gonna do the work, let alone even pick up a sledge-hammer.' And he said, 'I told you not to call me Pac-Man!'

"He walked up to my face, angrily looking at me. But I wasn't intim-idated one bit, and stood my ground. 'Or what, Pac-Man, you gonna hit me? I don't think you could, because that would actually require you to lift a finger. SOMETHING YOU'VE NEVER DONE ONCE IN YOUR WHOLE LIFE!'

"Once I said this, Packer angrily grunted and shoved me against the hardwood wall. He grabbed the sledgehammer and ran towards me. He threw the sledgehammer back, ready to swing, and once he swung, I dove down, narrowly missing his swing into the wood. Once he noticed I was on the ground, he removed the sledgehammer from the wall and prepared to strike me while I was on the ground. Again he narrowly missed as I dodged and rolled out of his way. After that, I jumped up to a standing position, and he just kept on swinging at me as I backed up. Left, right, left, right, it was just continuous swinging. With each swing, he just barely missed me. I could feel the rush of air across my face each time he swung. But pretty soon his swings got slower and slower, and so did his movement.

"After one final swing, he collapsed to a kneeling position with his sledgehammer for support. But then he looked up, and angrily looked at me again, he was ready to get up and swing some more. But I wasn't gonna let that happen. As soon as he got up, I grabbed him by the throat and struck him in the face. He immediately fell down and started bleeding from his nose. I was even pulling my punch. That construction job made me really strong. Imagine if I did use all my might, it could have been a lot worse for him.

"Soon after, the manager came running and yelled, 'What's going on?!' I told him I defended myself, and he could have easily killed me if one of his swings had landed. My other coworkers jumped in and vouched for me, all supporting me in unison. Though I wished those cowards would have just as easily jumped in to help me.

"My manager was stunned for a moment, but then just said, 'Get out. You're fired.'

"'Good riddance. Good luck working here while your hardest worker is gone,' and then I walked away. I threw aside my hard hat and other PPE. As I walked away, I could overhear Packer and the manager talking.

"'Packer, you're fired too. I'm tired of carrying you around here.'

"'I'm gonna call the cops. I'm gonna sue. I'm gonna . . . '

"'You go right ahead. That's gonna end up worse for you, since you just tried to kill a man and there's witnesses. You're done here, Packer.'

"So it seems my day was a lot more eventful than yours."

We both burst into laughter. It was a genuine moment of connection, where we could relate to each other's struggles and appreciate our shared sense of humor. It was a rare moment, as my dad and I barely conversed about anything. But that story showed the best parts of him, all the parts that I desired to be. I admired my dad for his witticisms and his clever comebacks, but mostly his power to stand up to anyone and not be crushed by those around him. I wanted to be like that someday.

The car ride the rest of the way was pretty lighthearted. We joked about numerous things we found irritating, but mostly the dumb and imperfect people who got in our way. I told him how it was funny that many of my classmates encouraged me to step out of my shell and socialize with others. But every time I tried to socialize with someone, I was met with disappointment.

I remember I was invited to a party near the start of the school year at a classmate's house. The classmate was the class president, and he tried to be friends with everyone. Well, everyone besides me. I thought a cordial invitation was an attempt at friendship, but it was a lazy attempt. When I arrived, the house's basement bustled with noise from a crowd. But it lacked any lighting, as if the crowd itself reveled in the shadows, desperate to escape the shadow of their own lives. I approached the class president while he was mingling around, and tried to engage in a conversation with him.

"Hey! Thanks for inviting me to this."

"We would have missed you if you didn't show."

Oh, I'm sure.

"So tell me, Robbie, what plans do you have this weekend?"

"Probably a lot of reading. I'm currently reading Plato's *Republic* and its thoughts on justice. I've just started, but it seems to criticize the idea of justice being the advantage of the stronger. Or to put it simply, justice being determined by those in power and what is popular. There must be more to life than following the ordinary feelings of conformity or a desire to fit in. One should try to escape the cave you live in, even if you're alone . . . So, I'm doing some really light reading. Hahahaha."

"That's . . . cool . . . Oh, look, some other guests are here and I better introduce myself."

And then he quickly walked away, leaving me alone. I tried to converse with him the rest of the night. I thought that since he invited me that he wanted to befriend me, but I guess not. If he didn't want me here, then why did he invite me? Did he think that simply inviting me to a party was enough?

I then tried to converse with the rest of the crowd, but it resulted in the same outcome every conversation. So then after some frustration, I walked out of the party. I won't recount every time I tried to approach someone in my life, but no matter what approach I took, the approach I took was always wrong. Trying to converse with anyone my age was like trying to drive through a brick wall; it was pointless. At least you could eventually drive through a brick wall.

Yet paradoxically, classmates would still approach me, just not to befriend me. They distanced themselves from me, labeling me as the class freak, yet they never hesitated to seek my assistance when they needed it. In one instance, while the class was doing an in-class activity, I overheard one girl saying to another girl that she'd rather slash her wrists than ask me to a Sadie Hawkins dance. I don't know how she thought she was being quiet; I could overhear that remark from across the room. But afterwards, I easily completed a simple worksheet. I glanced around the classroom to find my peers frantically scouring the internet for answers.

The same girl who scornfully dismissed the idea of going to a dance with me approached my desk. She had a question, one that she couldn't simply Google on her phone. She handed me the worksheet, pointing to a particular query: 'What is the definition of irony?' The moment I read those words, I broke out into uncontrollable laughter. Confused, she asked what was so funny. I responded that irony is mocking your classmates and then desperately asking them for help. I could tell that wounded her a bit, but I was oblivious to her feelings, as she was to mine. It was staggering to believe I could meet someone so imperfectly stupid. But then I remember other moments, and I realize I met those people often. Moments like these would continue, resulting in fewer classmates asking me for help, which I preferred.

I recounted these incidents to my dad, and a genuine laugh escaped his lips. It was another moment of shared amusement. By the time we reached home, pulling into the garage, something caught my eye. Near the side of the garage was a bicycle. Its dark black frame, untouched for years, seemed strangely preserved, with tires that hadn't deflated over time. It was my mom's old bicycle. Memories flooded my mind, memories of a time when she would ride it frequently. My mom seemed to ride the wheels of life flawlessly, just like this bicycle. But as her battle with cancer intensified, her rides became less frequent, until she could no longer use it.

I remember how I used to run up to her, brimming with excitement, asking, "Mommy, can I ride the big wheels? When can I ride the big wheels?"

That was my nickname for the bike—the big wheels. It always filled me with hope and happiness. I yearned for the day when my mom would teach me how to ride it. But that day never came. As her rides diminished, so did my thoughts of the bicycle. I couldn't help but feel a pang of sadness and wonder if it had become too painful for my mom to look at, and that's why it was shoved in the corner. It seemed these memories had a penchant for overpowering me while I was behind the wheel. But I realized, at that moment, that I never learned how to ride that bike. It was a simple skill every privileged person should know how to do.

I turned around and asked my dad, "Hey, you never did teach me how to ride this. Do you think you can show me now?"

"Not now, Robbie," he said, walking inside.

I was a little put down with his disinclination, but I was undeterred. Rolling the bike into the street, I sought more space to learn. I had a vague idea of riding a bike. I knew that I had to keep moving to maintain stability, but putting it into practice proved far more challenging. As soon as I got both feet on the pedals, I'd have trouble maintaining balance. So to mitigate this effect, I thought I'd get the bike moving first and then start pedaling. With this in mind, I started moving the bike and tried to get on it after enough speed, which immediately resulted in me falling over with the bike on top of me. After a second attempt, I gave it even more speed, but this time I fell on top of the bike. Next I tried while it was stationary, but I was unable to balance myself after many attempts, with each attempt ending with me putting my leg down to stop the bike from falling.

The last attempt ended with me taking too long to pedal and the bike falling on me again. At that point I started to get frustrated and thought maybe I just wasn't doing it at a fast enough speed. So with the bike in my hands, I charged forward with all my might and jumped on the bike to try and start pedaling the wheels. But before I could, the bike started maneuvering out of control and I crashed into the curb, taking a nosedive and rolling over two or three times on the concrete.

After my last roll, I was lying face up, cuts and bruises all over my arms. My face was bleeding profusely, but I didn't care. I just wanted to lie there and wallow in my own defeated state. Then I overheard some bicyclists riding by. I looked up and saw two Black boys half my age.

I could hear one of them say, "Look at this white boy, doesn't even know how to ride a bike."

The other replied, "Never seen anyone so white in my life."

Then they both just pedaled their wheels away in laughter. This only added to my agony.

I tried, and I tried again and again in so many ways. But I just couldn't turn the big wheels.

GONE WITH THE WIND

Yesterday. What a day. The falls left me with aches and pains that radiated through every inch of my body. As I surveyed the cuts and bruises on my arms and face, a wave of frustration and disappointment washed over me. My dad didn't even notice, leaving me to clean up my wounds alone. The physical pain couldn't compare to the emotional sting of his indifference. The car ride now felt like a world away, and I couldn't grasp the connection.

But then, as the school bell resounded through the air, class commenced. It was my Spanish class, and I was primed and prepared. The pride in my work was one of the few moments of happiness I could lean on in school. With my trusty ebony writing pen, crimson correcting pen, and diligently completed homework arranged neatly on my desk, I was ready to dive in. Meanwhile, my classmates were not ready. They lagged behind, still extracting their belongings and engaged in casual chatter, while I patiently occupied my seat, nestled within the esteemed ranks of the honors class. Our numbers were limited, and the room was neatly divided into three distinct rows. I was situated in the middle row, occupying the second desk from the front. The vacant desk before me, normally occupied by a perpetually tardy girl, beckoned for her arrival. And right on cue, just as the classroom hushed and the teacher commenced her rounds to inspect our homework, she finally appeared. She was tall, but built, her physique a harmonious blend of strength and grace that exuded effortless elegance. With her shoulders back and head held high, she radiated a self-confident aura that drew everyone's eyes for every room she walked in. I watched as she sauntered into the classroom, her carefree demeanor contrasting with the seriousness of the honors class.

I must admit, she held the advantage of being older than me and possessed a captivating allure. With her cascading tresses of straight, sunset-red hair, she rivaled the most beautiful actresses gracing our screens today. However, beyond her aesthetic appeal, I hadn't formed much of an impression of this girl based on my limited interactions. In the few classes we shared so far, her perpetual tardiness and occasional lengthy absences during bathroom breaks stood out. It appeared to me that she didn't place much importance on her education, a characteristic flaw that, while disconcerting, seemed all too prevalent within the school's student body. I couldn't discern any exceptional qualities that set her apart from the multitude of faces I would come across.

As the teacher approached my desk, she directed her attention towards me with a gentle reminder. "Robbie, do you recall our discussion on the very first day about stapling your homework?"

I looked at my homework, and became acutely aware of the fact that my worksheet pages remained unstapled. The tumbles I had experienced yesterday seemed to have shaken loose my recollection of homework protocol. I reached for the pages and attempted to rise from my seat, heading towards the stapler stationed on the teacher's desk at the rear of the classroom. However, a searing ache emanating from the cuts and bruises on my body forced me to relinquish the pages, causing them to scatter haphazardly across the floor. I strained to bend down and retrieve them, but the excruciating pain that coursed through me with each movement rendered me powerless. It was as if the simple act of picking up a single sheet of paper exacted an unbearable toll.

It was then that the girl seated in front of me recognized my struggle and placed a comforting hand upon my shoulder. With genuine concern on her face, she asked, "Wow, are you okay? Do you need some help?"

Grateful for her offer, I reluctantly nodded. But I couldn't help but argue against her selflessness, insisting that she shouldn't have to go through the trouble on my behalf. Yet she remained resolute, and repeated her offer to help. Eventually, realizing her genuine zeal, I yielded and settled back into my seat as the girl took charge, skillfully gathering all my scattered pages and stapling them securely.

As the teacher's gaze fell upon my visible bruises, concern etched across her face, she inquired about my well-being. I waved away her concern, asserting that I was perfectly fine. Accepting my reassurance, she moved on to check my homework and the girl's. With the teacher momentarily occupied, the girl turned in her seat, facing me directly.

"Next time, just ask, alright? I'd be more than happy to help," she offered, her voice laced with sincerity.

I mustered a simple "thank you" in response.

Curiosity gleamed in her eyes, "What happened to you?"

I smirked and playfully coughed twice, explaining, "Well, you won't believe it. Yesterday, I was out for a leisurely stroll on my street, when out of nowhere a tiger leapt upon me, its claws tearing at my flesh. She took off in a flash, leaving me to chase after her. But no matter how fast I ran, she eluded me, always a few strides ahead. But don't worry, this is a regular thing for me."

Her eyes widened in amusement and she began to laugh. Her laughter resonated through the air, reaching deep within me in a way that surpassed any previous social interaction I had experienced, surpassing even the moments shared with Lauro or Maddy. The sight of her smile was a rarity, one of those unforgettable, once-in-a-lifetime smiles. What made it truly special was that it was actually an honest smile.

However, our laughter was soon interrupted as class resumed. After reviewing the homework, our teacher instructed us to engage in a class activity for the remainder of the period. We were asked to ask questions in Spanish to the person next to us. Given no other options, I found myself partnered with the girl seated in front of me. Not that I minded, as our conversations had already begun to grow more enjoyable.

Turning to the page where I had written my questions, I noticed some grammatical errors in my vocabulary. Swiftly I crossed them out and corrected the words, prompting a memory from the day before. My dad had actually conversed with me.

While I was diligently working on my homework, my dad casually remarked, "I don't know how your teacher manages to read your handwriting. Hahaha!"

Reflecting on this, I rectified the errors in my homework. After some time, he asked me if I said I was going to hang out with anyone that night.

"No," I replied.

He smiled, shook his head, and asked me, "You're in high school. Aren't you supposed to be dating girls, or something besides staying home all night?"

Not knowing what to say, I tried ignoring him, and continued to focus on my homework.

And then after a few seconds, he said to me, "Why can't you be a normal person? Do you need psychological help?"

And those wounding words reminded me how distant I was with my dad. I tried to forget it like I tried to forget yesterday.

Kindness glowing from her eyes, the girl glanced at my paper and remarked, "You have really pretty handwriting."

"Oh no, it's nothing special, really," I replied modestly. "But let's get back to work. Sorry for the delay . . ." Following the teacher's instructions, I asked her, *"¿Qué harás en el futuro como un trabajo?"*

"Uhh . . . okay . . . crap . . . What did you just say?"

I replied, "I asked what you will do as a job in the future."

"Oh, *yo planeo ser una enfermera.*"

"Ahh, a nurse. Why do you want to do that?" I inquired, genuinely interested in her reasons.

"I just like to help people; I can't stand to see others struggling alone."

"That warms my heart. . . . .What's your question?"

"¿Planearás casarte en el futuro?" Her voice was gentle and curious.

"Hmmm . . . . *Sí e no*. You can't force marriage. If you find someone, you find someone, it's best not to force love."

"True!"

"Alright, let 's go again. *¿Qué harás en tu tiempo libre cuándo seas mayor?*" I asked.

"*Lo mismo . . .que . . .hago ahora . . .ver películas, hacer ejercicio, y pasar tiempo con amigas.*"

Intrigued, I said, "*Bueno*. You like to watch movies?"

"Very much so."

"And I mean really watch them? You don't just watch *Titanic* on repeat, do you?"

"Hahahaha. . . . Hey, don't tell me you don't tear up when Jack dies." Her laughter was music to my ears.

"I don't. I'm usually asleep by the time they actually get to the *Titanic*. I don't know how anyone can sit through the movie."

"What? How can you not love that story between Jack and Rose? Aren't you drawn in?"

"Romance stories are too fanciful and don't accurately capture the concept of love. I mean, to fall in love out of nowhere at random, pffft!"

"Wow, and I thought I had a rough childhood. Hahahaha . . . Hey, we're pretty much done, we don't have to keep going." A twinkle shone in her eyes.

"Well . . . uhh . . . we should follow the teacher's instructions."

She reached out and touched my arm gently. Her touch sent a jolt of electricity through me.

"Okay, I'll ask you one then. ¿Qué pasó ayer?"

I let out a sigh. "I tried . . . I tried to ride a bike."

"Really?" Her eyes widened in surprise.

"Yes. I thought everyone knew how to ride a bike, and . . . I wanted to be like everyone else."

She paused and looked me in the eyes. Her hand gently touched the cut on my face, her gaze filled with empathy, "Don't . . . just be you. I always admire someone who can just be themself. . . . And don't feel bad about your cuts, they don't make you any less . . . *guapo*."

Suddenly, the bell rang, or maybe it was my heart skipping a beat.

She quickly gathered her things and left, but not before giving a parting remark. "Be careful on the bike ride home. Oh wait, never mind. . . . Catch you later."

And at that moment, it felt like I had just fallen in love.

• • •

Yesterday was such an incredible day. I couldn't wait to see her again. Just as I was sitting in my seat, the bell rang, signaling the start of class. And there she was, making her entrance. She quickly sat in front of me, organizing her belongings. As she pulled out her homework, she turned back to me to ask a favor.

"Hey, can I take a look at your homework? There were a few answers I didn't get."

Glancing at the teacher, who was preoccupied with checking everyone's assignments, I handed over my homework to her. She quickly jotted down the answers, and I realized the worksheet problems weren't too challenging. Instead of judging her, I considered that she might have been dealing with some issues the previous day. So I chose to be understanding.

Once she finished, she returned the homework with gratitude.

"Thank you so much. You're a lifesaver!"

"Not a problem, Miss Sunshine." I replied with a smile.

"Hahaha. What's your name again?", her eyes sparkling with curiosity.

"Robbie Shelby. And yours?"

"Rachel Roberts. I'm surprised, I didn't think you were much of a talker."

"You might regret saying that. Now you might not be able to get me to shut up." This caused us both to laugh loudly.

The teacher made her way around the classroom, checking everyone's homework, including Rachel's and mine, then class officially began.

Our Spanish lesson focused on the topic of traveling, and at one point the teacher asked Rachel a question: "¿Te comunicarás con tus amigos cuando viajes?"

Rachel was stuck for a few seconds, visibly confused. I quietly whispered to her, "*Sí, me comunicaré con mis amigos.*"

She repeated my response and satisfied the teacher. She turned to me, thanked me, and class continued.

Soon enough, the teacher decided to end class early, and Rachel wasted no time turning around to start a conversation with me. It was an unexpected and captivating moment. I had never experienced someone so enthusiastic and eager to talk with me. It was so unusual yet so magnetic, someone so wide-eyed and high-pitched in their voice, expressing such interest to talk with me. No one had ever done that with me before, and it was perfect.

She turned to me and said, "Hey guess what movie I saw this weekend? *The Notebook.*"

"Of course you would see that movie. No surprise there."

"Oh shut up."

"Hey if you're really looking for a shirtless guy, why not just watch porn? It'd probably be more satisfying."

She punched me lightly on the shoulder, laughing. Then leaning in closer to my ear, she whispered, "Oh Robbie, those are my favorite types of movies."

We burst into laughter, our jokes and banter becoming a common thread in the class we shared daily. It was a connection I cherished. When the bell rang, we walked out together. Then she bid me farewell and took a few steps ahead, where she hugged and kissed another man. It stung a bit to see, and reminded me of yet another pathway that was blocked off to me. But I shrugged it off and moved on.

Heading to the lunchroom, I joined Maddy and Lauro at our usual table. However, I was starting to lose interest in sitting with them. Our conversations had become stagnant, revolving mostly around gossip and judgment of others. It bothered me how they focused on criticizing and making snap judgments about people, especially about whether they were mentally ill, as if they were experts. It lacked intellectual stimulation and was shallow. We were not doctors, after all. It wasn't our place to judge. As I sat there contemplating my friendships, I couldn't help but feel a longing for more meaningful connections and conversations.

Lauro interrupted my thoughts. "Hey Robbie, I know you like day-dreaming, but I have a question for you."

"Wow, you actually have an interest in me, Lauro. I'm flattered. What is it?"

"Word is going around that you're going after Rachel Roberts? That true? You know she has a boyfriend right?"

"What? No, we're just friends. . . . Word goes around fast here, huh?"

"Are you sure? Because a lot of people in your Spanish class have noticed you flirting with her the whole time."

"Yeah, Robbie," said Maddy, "You don't have a secret crush, do you?"

"It's not like that." And the topic was dropped.

As Maddy and Lauro quickly shifted their conversation to someone in our class whom they believed had autism, I couldn't help but be disappointed. It was disheartening to how easily they transitioned from discussing one person to another so casually. I couldn't help but wonder about the conversations they had when I wasn't around. I could only imagine what they might be saying about me. I longed for deeper connections, where conversations were meaningful and empathetic, rather than filled with judgment and gossip.

But as the school year passed, my conversations with Rachel became a daily highlight. No matter what kind of mood I was in or what happened the day before, she always managed to brighten my day. I couldn't recall every single conversation we had because the days seemed to blend together, filled with discussions about our shared interest in movies. Whether I was playfully teasing her about her favorite rom-coms or she was berating my obscure art-house film choices, we always managed to make each other laugh. And when she laughed, the smile on her face was the kind you could never forget.

Our relationship grew so much that we began to interact outside of class. One night, when I was just lying in bed, I received a message from Rachel on Snapchat, an app I seldom used.

She sent me a picture of herself sticking out her tongue with the caption "Hey, Robbie! I'm bored. Do you have any good movie suggestions?"

Equally surprised and delighted to see her message, I responded with a film that was more my taste but I thought she would find appealing. "Have you seen *Eternal Sunshine of the Spotless Mind*?"

She replied that she hadn't seen it, and I began to dissect why it was a great film. Many nights like these began to follow. I vividly recalled messaging Rachel as the time ticked away into the night, my phone illuminating the darkness as we exchanged messages. It was as if a virtual bond emerged, our screens bridging the physical distance between us. Most of our interactions followed the pattern of recommending each other films to watch, eager to explore cinematic worlds. Her messages appeared on my screen like a whisper in the dark, and I responded with equal enthusiasm, suggesting hidden gems or critical darlings that had left an indelible mark on my soul.

As we delved into discussions about our favorite directors, mesmerizing performances, and captivating cinematography, our connection deepened. Rachel didn't have much experience with the nuts and bolts of film, but I was happy to teach her. In these moments, lying in our separate beds, we were united in our shared love for the magic of cinema.

"You see the close-ups on the actors' faces are meant to emphasize the emotion and connection the two of them have," I messaged Rachel.

"Oh wow, I didn't think of it like that . . . I was just more impressed with the actors' performances. The way she cried at the ending, and gave it all she had really stood out to me," she replied.

But sometimes, our conversations would veer beyond movie recommendations. We'd share snippets of our lives and glimpses into our souls.

"I'm going to be traveling to Hawaii next week for spring break. Wish me luck! Sometimes I wish I could live there," Rachel messaged me.

"Oh, so you travel and enjoy being outside then, huh?"

"I do. It's so much fun when I'm out and about. Lately at night, I try to find things to do to keep my mind active before I fall asleep. Sometimes I get so anxious when I'm at home."

"Except when you're talking to me right?!"

"Absolutely!"

These nights of exchanging messages, lying side by side in our sanctuary of sheets and thoughts, became precious to me. They were fleeting moments of intimacy, where we bared our souls through words and the flickering glow of our screens. We forged a connection that transcended the physical distance between us.

• • •

As the year continued to pass, an exchange in our Spanish class between Rachel and me stuck out to me.

"Hey, Robbie!"

"Hey, Rachel! How's you and your boyfriend?"

"Good. . . . How's you and the girls?"

"Do you even have to ask?"

"Yes, because they never talk about you."

"Oh, haha . . . ."

Rachel continued, "I wanted to ask you. You give me a hard time for my taste in movies. So, let's hear it from you. What's your favorite . . . . romantic movie?"

"Hmm . . . I'd have to say . . . *Shakespeare in Love*."

"Huh? How can you call yourself a movie buff and love that movie? That movie is literally criticized so much."

"Well . . . I just relate a lot to the wish fulfillment of that movie. . . . Every genius needs a lover."

Rachel laughed. "Haha. Well, this is rich. Are you a genius then?"

"Shakespeare's got nothing on me."

"Hahahaha. Wow, so modest."

"Modesty is not in my vocabulary, and my vocabulary is pretty far-reaching."

After a pause, Rachel changed the subject. It reminded me of other moments when she seemed to briefly narrow her eyebrows. But I brushed it off, assuming it was nothing important.

I continued, "I don't know . . . maybe I'll be a writer . . . filmmaker . . . something I can leave my creative stamp on. I may or may not have a broken heart, and that will allow me to create some of the greatest stories ever told. So you know, just the usual tortured genius."

Rachel's response was a bit underwhelming, and for a split second, she narrowed her eyebrows. But I quickly moved on, not dwelling on it. She then asked about plans for the summer.

"Maybe I'll go watch some movies at the theater. Want to come watch one with me? We definitely should hang out sometime."

"Yes. Sure."

Her response lacked the usual enthusiasm. It dawned on me that this was the last day of classes, the last time I'd be seeing her . . . for class, I mean. But I remained hopeful that I would see her over the summer and the year afterwards. And as soon as the bell rang, we both got up from our desks, she hugged me with that one-of-a-kind smile, and then she left.

43

• • •

I remembered the day with vivid vehemence, as if it had happened yes-terday. I stood outside the movie theater, waiting for Rachel, anticipation building with every fleeting moment. Gusts of wind breezed across my face, whispering reminders that this moment was slipping through my fingers. A bustling crowd surged around me, a restless tide of faces and laughter, yet I felt suspended in time. Then her car glided into the parking lot, like a bright lighthouse on a stormy night. As she stepped out of the vehicle and rushed towards me, her presence seemed to illuminate every-thing around her. She wore a pair of jeans that fitted her body perfectly, paired with a crisp white blouse that flowed elegantly with her move-ments. She hugged me gracefully, exclaiming my name using all her lungs. I didn't want to let go and, it seemed, that neither did she.

It was near the end of summer, and my sophomore year of high school was about to begin. In the summer, we didn't really message each other as much as we used to. I sometimes tried to message her, but she would always say she was too busy. I would check her social media page, and it was usually filled with pictures of her boyfriend and herself. It sad-dened me a little, but I thought nothing of it at the time, thinking that we'd still be close.

By pure coincidence, I decided to send Rachel a random picture of myself through Snapchat. Surprisingly, she responded and we started a conversation. That's when I learned that she had broken up with her boy-friend. Seizing the opportunity, I asked her if she wanted to hang out, and her enthusiastic response made me realize the potential double meaning of my invitation.

I asked her if she considered it a date, to which she responded, "What do you want it to be?"

With all honesty, I told her, "It can be whatever you want it to be, because either way is fine with me."

And that led me there, on my first date ever, with a person who brought me never-ending joy.

As we walked towards the movie theater entrance, we started talking and she revealed that she was switching schools. I retorted that it broke my heart a little, because who was gonna converse with me about movies now, who was gonna converse with me at all?

She responded, "I don't know," but with her smile, at least I thought so.

While walking inside the theater, I asked her, "Why are you switching schools?"

Rachel sighed and ran her fingers through her hair, her eyes no longer twinkling, but weary. "I've just been feeling stuck here, you know? It just felt like I was missing out on something more, something that could empower me."

Inside the theater, Rachel suggested taking a Snapchat together, and we did. Every time she took a picture, she would have a unique expression, sticking out her tongue and raising her eyebrows in a distinctive way. She checked her phone often during the date, and I playfully nudged her when a commercial about no cell phone use during the movie played. It got her laughing, and seeing her smile made me smile too. She sat to my left, and I noticed that she didn't put up her armrest. I briefly contemplated putting my arm around her, but I hesitated, lacking the courage to make that move on our first date. It was a moment I often look back on.

The movie we watched was my suggestion, a reshowing of the classic film *Gone with the Wind*. Rachel had never seen it before, and I believed that if she truly loved movies, she had to experience it. As soon as the movie ended, she expressed how sad it was, particularly the ending where someone who meant so much to someone else could disappear like the wind, leaving only memories behind.

"That's just so sad, Robbie."

Our conversation continued over dinner at a restaurant I thought she would enjoy. I can't recall the details of what we discussed, but it was typical small talk—our classes, family life, and other everyday topics. It was hard to accept, but perhaps we weren't laughing as much as we used to. It didn't seem like I was acting any different. What was I doing wrong? Nevertheless, after dinner, she drove me home, I hugged her tightly, and then she drove away.

• • •

Then the memory ended. I never saw her again. It lingered and etched into my mind with bittersweet intensity. Finally I reached the final year of high school, when life was filled with uncertainty. I found myself seated at the back of my Spanish class, lost in thoughts of Rachel and yearning for conversations we used to have. Despite my ability to communicate fluently in Spanish, I would have given it all up in an instant just to relive those moments with her. It sounded foolish, but I couldn't help it. I couldn't get her out of my head.

I thought that what we had was irreplaceable. It had meant the world to me, and I thought it held the same significance for her. I thought. But as the years went by, doubts started to creep in, and I began questioning if she truly cared for me as much as it felt. I would often look back on our time together and wonder if I had misinterpreted everything. Maybe I had imagined a connection that wasn't really there. But why did she agree to go on a date with me? Why did she laugh and enjoy our time together? Was it all just an act? I couldn't bring myself to believe that.

Perhaps the fact that she attended a different high school played a role in the distance that grew between us. Communication became harder, and despite my attempts to reach out to her, she gradually stopped responding. She vanished into thin air, leaving me with unanswered questions and a lingering ache in my heart.

Occasionally, I would browse my phone and go back to the picture that we took at the movie theater, a moment frozen in time. I delved into the depths of our physiognomic expressions, lost in a flood of heart-rending nostalgia. It was us, smiling and carefree, our laughter echoing through a bundle of other memories. But the connection faded away like a gust of wind breezing by. I decided to delete the photo, but it did nothing to temper the despair, nor did the memory fade away any less.

As such, when I would go to bed, I'd lie awake into the wee small hours of the night, consumed by thoughts of Rachel. I would ponder what could have been, questioning if things could have turned out differently if I had been different somehow. Did she ever think about me as much as I thought about her? But as the years passed, I observed her in pictures with another man, and then another, and then another. It took time, but I realized she probably didn't dwell about yesterday as much as I did, and that realization hurt my heart the most.

ANOTHER BRICK IN THE WALL

"Remember students, you are loved," echoed the final announcement on the high school PA.

Of course we were. They repeated it every morning, with even more enthusiasm than the Pledge of Allegiance. Remember, just repeat a lie multiple times, and maybe someone will believe you. Maybe you'll even believe it yourself.

The teacher was absent from the room, leaving me alone at the front desk, lost in my thoughts. Or at least trying to be lost in thought. The classroom was filled with girls clustering in the back, like a flock of birds unable to be alone. The senseless drivel that they began to blather out of their mouths was suffocating.

"It was so big. Admit it, you'd love to suck it too."

"But he's really weird. I can't hold a conversation with him. He constantly changes the subject constantly for no reason. Talking to him makes me feel uncomfortable. He probably has ADHD."

"But he's a basketball captain. If you hook up with him, imagine what it could do to your reputation."

"Yeah. I mean, I can always just ghost him when I want to, right?"

What kind of person do you have to be to go along with this? I longed for a conversation that held substance, and went beyond the superficiality I was consistently exposed to.

Suddenly, Ms. Blackwell entered the room.

"Robbie, may I talk to you for a minute?"

"About?"

She then motioned me to join her. I followed her to her empty classroom, devoid of students but filled with the usual political propaganda. I settled in a desk, pulling it up close towards hers. I shrugged my hands, demanding an answer why she interrupted one of my classes.

"Robbie, a student came to me deeply concerned about a poem you shared in class."

"It was called 'Eclipse' by Pink Floyd. I didn't write it. The assignment was to present a poem in class, song lyrics were included. . . . And I'm not surprised. You can search me if you want. I'm not carrying any firearms."

"We were just concerned about you. What was the poem even about?"

"It was about layers of trauma, and how, like the moon, it can eclipse your sanity. Why would someone approach you about this?"

Ms. Blackwell narrowed her eyebrows. "Because people feel comfortable sharing things with me. It's something you should learn how to do. And you can start by not feeling comfortable sharing things with others."

"Why? Why am I not allowed to express myself?"

"Because most people shouldn't share creepy poems. It's not normal. It's not what everyone else does."

"Why would I want to be like everyone else? Art is meant to challenge the status quo, not conform to it."

Ms. Blackwell sighed. "Robbie, you should look into seeing a therapist. It could really help you in understanding your interactions with others."

"Okay . . ." I lacked the power to respond and continue the exchange.

She shifted the conversation and started sharing details about her life. Eventually, I left the room and tried to leave the conversation behind.

As the day progressed, lunchtime finally arrived, and I plodded along into the lunchroom. I sat at a table full of people, but as soon as I sat down, they gathered their things and left, expressing annoyance. I closed my eyes, silently sitting there, fed up with the animals I was forced to encounter every day. It was like I was imprisoned, trapped with the most degenerate scum of the earth. This was a private high school, but it hardly contained an educated community as advertised. Half the school was filled with criminals, and the other half spoiled rich kids. Theft was rampant. They drank, and they fucked, and they smoked, and they talked about it, and then they did it all over again. Again, again, and again. They were a bunch of debauched beasts, incapable of anything above primal instinct.

I opened my eyes, and glanced around, taking in the chaotic scene that unfolded before my eyes. Tables filled with students engaged in reckless behaviors, fueled by a potent mix of rebellion and peer pressure.

At one table, students openly passed around small bags, their contents undoubtedly containing more than harmless lunches. The distinct smell of marijuana mingled with the scent of cafeteria food, creating an unsettling combination. But the bags would often contain more than one type of drug. Probably every type of narcotic was exchanged in that lunchroom. Laughter and hushed whispers accompanied each transaction, as if the shared enjoyment only fueled their excitement.

At another table, a group of boys and girls seemed oblivious to the world around them, each pair locked in an embrace that left little to the imagination. Their hands roamed freely, their actions brazen and publicly unapologetic. Then the pairs would change and they would begin another embrace. It was as if decency dissolved within the lunchroom walls, replaced by a reckless desire for instant gratification.

I caught glimpses of stolen glances and secret smiles, the unspoken agreements between classmates engaged in hidden trysts and clandestine alliances. It seemed as though conformity had taken front seat, coinciding with a relentless pursuit of pleasure and acceptance, even if it meant sacrificing personal values and integrity.

Once again I was an outsider in this twisted theater, where the lines of morality blurred, and the desire to fit in eclipsed any sense of individuality.

It was a constant reminder of what humanity had to offer, a stark contrast to the innocence and purity of my younger years.

As I observed the debauchery unfolding around me, I realized that this was the world I was expected to embrace, the world I was supposed to conform to. It was a disheartening realization, one that made me question whether I could find my place amidst the chaos, or if this would forever just be another brick in the wall.

As I was lost in my thoughts, Maddy and Lauro approached and sat down with me, their smiles warm and welcoming. But behind their friendly facade, I couldn't help but question their intentions. Did they truly accept me for who I was, or did they only value my presence as long as I conformed to their expectations?

"We saw that you were lonely over here, so we thought we'd come and say hello," said Lauro.

"Well . . . hello."

"Hahahaha . . . Hey, Robbie, remember when you were fooling around with Rachel Roberts? How did that end with her again?"

I sighed. "I don't want to discuss that. How's lacrosse going?"

"Not good. We haven't won a single game. I got injured in the last game, so I can't help the team out that much. But who cares? I don't really want to win. None of the guys do. We're just going through the motions, waiting for the season to be over."

"Didn't you get injured last year as well?"

"I've gotten injured every year since I've been playing sports. Sometimes I even skip practice to make sure I don't get injured."

"One might argue that you're not as tough as you think."

He grimaced and rose from his chair a little. "Hey! I'm tougher than anyone else on that team. You're not playing; you don't understand. I'm the captain, voted in by the team, that's what matters."

I shut my eyes, and was unable to gather the strength to pursue the exchange. "Whatever you say. I apologize."

"Easy there, Lauro," Maddy interjected, "Robbie makes a good point. Maybe you should . . . commit to your team more."

"Maybe you should practice what you preach, Maddy. How is your nonprofit organization for underprivileged women?"

"It's hard because . . . I'm so busy. It's hard to make time when I have so many other interests."

"Like what?" I asked.

"Well, me and Lauro like to party . . .

I understood that as an euphemism for drinking and doing drugs, almost as if saying that out loud was committing a faux pas.

"And I mean, I have to party. That's what everyone else does every week. I have to fit in. I don't want to be perceived as weird."

Lauro jumped in, "But you should commit to your teammates more.'"

Maddy continued, "But it doesn't help that some of my teammates are toxic, leaving me emotionally drained and anxious. There's this one narcissistic girl that doesn't like to party. She's so conceited; I bet she thinks she's so much better than us."

Lauro commented, "Oh you mean Britney? I hate her so much."

"She's such a bitch . . ."

At a loss for words, I remained silent. Maddy noticed my disinterest.

"Hey, do you wanna come to a party this weekend, Robbie?"

They exchanged glances before looking at me. But before I could answer, she asked me another question, yet she was so nervous that she couldn't maintain eye contact.

"Robbie . . . I have a close friend who lost her dad. . . . and she said therapy really helped her get through it. . . ."

It dawned on me that this was just another typical day in high school. Every single day, I was reminded of the worst that humanity had to offer. And every single day, I was reminded that I needed to conform to it.

Out of irritation, I gathered my belongings and left. As the day dragged on, I couldn't focus on any of my classes. My mind was consumed by the gossip circulating around me, but not as sugarcoated as Maddy would put it.

As the day ended, I walked out of the school, grateful to escape. But almost instantaneously, Maddy and Lauro both texted a message to me, "Remember, Robbie, I care about you."

STEP OUT

"What are you reading these days, Robbie?" Maddy inquired.

"I'm currently perusing *The Outsiders*."

"What's it about?"

"It revolves around a group of friends who stick together through thick and thin, and the various challenges they face."

"Oh, like us!"

I was silent for a second, but responded, "Yes, of course."

Maddy continued, "Wait, isn't that one about a group of boys? Don't you realize how many stories revolve around the male perspective? Women have trouble connecting with stories like that."

I replied, "It's like when I read *Jane Eyre*, the first thing I do is imagine her being a man, because I can't possibly connect to it otherwise."

Maddy laughed and rolled her eyes. We were seated across from each other in a booth at Joe Schmoe's, a dimly lit bar with few bright lights allowing patrons to see. The central area housed a large circular counter, surrounded by shelves stocked with various alcoholic beverages. A small stage rested in the back, where people could sing karaoke, most of the time terribly. But besides that, the bar was bustling with noise, with the lively chatter outweighing the music playing. Almost every booth and bar stool was filled. And there was a long line of people waiting to sing with their terrible voices.

Maddy, Lauro, and I all graduated high school a couple weeks ago, and they wanted to celebrate. Although we were underage, they had fake IDs, and hooked me up with one. It wasn't like it mattered anyway. Plenty of my peers at my high school frequented the bar without any trouble. I overheard one classmate claim that they'd attended the bar since the age of fourteen. So it was more likely that the bar staff didn't care who they let in. They didn't want to turn down paying customers, no matter how old the customer was.

I was incredibly tempted not to go. But then it occurred to me that I rarely spoke to Maddy or Lauro outside of school. To an outsider, one might mistake us for not being friends at all. So I wanted to step out of my shell, for better or worse—hopefully not for the worse.

Maddy wore a gray jacket that wasn't zipped all the way. I noticed a rash on the left side of Maddy's neck.

I asked, "Hey Maddy, what's that gash you have on your neck?"

She immediately zipped up her jacket so the rash wasn't visible.

"Oh . . . Lauro gave that to me."

"What? Why? How?"

"That's none of your business, Robbie. Please respect my boundaries."

I countered, "Huh? Why should I respect your 'boundaries'?"

She replied, "Because I don't want to feel uncomfortable."

I was about to respond, but Lauro then came back from his bathroom break and rejoined Maddy. They instantly started chattering away, so I decided to let our exchange slip by. They delved into their usual gossip about others, and how glad they weren't ever going to talk to some of their schoolmates again. Both of them seemingly went through a list of each person, commenting on each one, as if they kept detailed notes about the mental disorders of every person they met.

As they were prattling, I lost track of their conversation and stared in the darkness, looking for a light. Lauro looked at me for a second, then quickly looked around the room.

"Robbie, you have to step out of your shell. See that girl over there? Go and talk to her."

Turning in his chair, Lauro pointed out a girl at the bar counter, dressed in a leather jacket and jeans, with short black hair cascading to her jaw. The stool next to her was empty.

"I'm supposed to just approach someone, really?"

"Yes, this is how making friends works."

I sighed, then I sighed again. I kept alternating my gaze between Lauro and Maddy and the woman. Despite my prolonged hesitation, Lauro repeatedly directed me with his eyes. It occurred to me that I needed to try to step out. I needed to do something different if I no longer wanted to reside on the outside of society. I sighed one final time, and lacked the power resist any longer. I squeezed out of the booth, and slowly approached the woman.

She remained facing forward as I neared her. I finally sat down at the stool next to her, and before I even uttered a sentence, she quickly stated, "Nope. Not today. I have enough friends."

I was gobsmacked, my mouth hanging open for several seconds. But I eventually closed it, and rose from the stool. Once again, I couldn't turn the big wheels.

I was about to walk away, but not before stating, "Me too."

I quickly walked back to Maddy and Lauro's booth, sitting back down.

"I take it you didn't make much of an impression," Lauro quipped.

"You are an astute observer, Lauro."

"Well, what are you doing here? Go back over there."

"Well, she said no, and I have to respect that, don't I?"

Maddy glared at Lauro, almost baiting him to disagree.

"Well, you see, Robbie," Lauro replied, "Women don't always mean what they say."

Maddy, of course, rolled her eyes and threw her hands in the air in disgust.

"I could say the same thing about men, mind you," Maddy added.

"I would agree," Lauro retorted.

"You know how Maddy and I got together, Robbie?"

"Was it love at first sight?"

Lauro laughed. "Almost . . . what happened was that our high school football team won a game. It was a semi-final game, and we were stacked to lose. We had countless injuries, and were using backup players to play. But through some miracle, we actually won. We played our hearts out and pushed the game into overtime. Through a lucky pass, we scored a last-minute touchdown to win. The team and the student section were all overjoyed. To celebrate, we immediately hosted a party at a friend's house. And guess who was at that party? Maddy. I didn't know Maddy very well, but I decided to walk up to her and see where things could go. Months and months earlier, I approached Maddy at another party, and she rejected me then. But I decided to approach again, nonetheless. We immediately hit it off, and . . . well . . . nothing much more to say really. Other than that, in order to get a good relationship, you have to put yourself out there."

I refrained from making a joke, and said something I should have said a while ago. "I was about to make a joke, but I just wanted to say guys, now that we've graduated high school, you two were the best part about it. I know I never expressed it, but I always appreciated how you two were there to be my friend."

Lauro stated, "Wow, that might be the nicest thing that came out of your mouth."

I laughed—it was true. Looking back on my high school years, much of my time was spent with Maddy and Lauro at lunch. Despite their frequent gossip, they were by my side.

Maddy interjected, "Yeah, Robbie, Lauro will agree with this. We have always valued you. Lauro and I have other friends beside you, but none of them are as honest as you. At times, Lauro and I feel like we're walking on eggshells with our other friends. It is exhausting trying to maintain friendships with them because we can't show how we really feel in front of them. It's why we always were around you, because we didn't have to worry about telling you our feelings."

I pondered her words. I hadn't considered their perspectives before. I hadn't considered that their expression of gossip was merely an outlet for their other friendships.

I immediately responded, "Well, you're welcome. I'm glad I'm of some use to somebody!"

We all laughed. We laughed until Lauro looked back at that woman and said, "Hey, you two stay here. Let me work some magic for you, Robbie."

He immediately jumped out of the booth and confidently walked over to the woman. Despite his lack of willpower, Lauro did have confidence.

"Tonight was good," Maddy remarked. "We should have more moments like this."

"As long as you're there!"

Lauro walked back to our booth, but with the woman at the bar closely following him.

"Robbie and Maddy, this is Rebecca. Rebecca, please sit. Maddy, let's give Rebecca and Robbie some privacy."

Maddy got out of the booth, and Rebecca immediately took her place.

"You two have fun now," and Lauro and Maddy strutted away.

At first, we both were silent. I was the first to break the silence.

"So what do you know? I guess 'no' does mean 'yes,' as evidenced by you sitting over here."

"Oh, I don't really want to be here. But your friend there paid me $50 to talk with you."

Wow, Lauro. Wow.

"I see. So I guess that makes you no better than a prostitute?"

She rolled her eyes. "I'm going to take a wild guess that you haven't been with any women before, let alone talked with them. Maybe you'd have some better luck if you were a little nicer?"

I quipped back, "Let me put this in a way you would understand: a man doesn't owe you a smile."

She laughed out loud when I said that to her. But she quickly stopped, as if the laugh was unintentional. She still had a smile on her face, though. In a way, I sort of admired her. She had a wit to her that was uncommon. In a leap of faith, I decided to further the conversation.

"So, what do you like to do? Besides going to bars?"

"Well, I am an active sort of person. So I go to the gym, and reject men's advances. I go to the swimming pool, and reject men's advances. And I go to the climbing gym, and reject men's advances."

"Well, how would you like to be approached then? The reason I walked up to you is because my friend goaded me into approaching you, because I don't have any friends besides them, or a girlfriend. So obviously I'm expected to step out. But you're telling me stepping out is problematic. So I ask again, how would you like me to approach you?"

She was silent for a while, but eventually said, "I don't know."

I gestured my hands to communicate the contradiction.

"Have you tried therapy?"

Here we go.

"No, I haven't."

"Well, you see, communication should be obvious. It's not hard to say the right words. If it is, therapy can help you get there."

I frustratingly inquired, "Why is it obvious? What are the right words?"

"Therapy can help you find that out."

"No. Don't try to walk away from the point. How am I expected to step out? What is the correct way to do that?"

Again, she shook her head, threw her hands in the air, and stated, "I don't know."

I also threw my hands in the air in discontent.

Rebecca asked, "I'm assuming you're against therapy. Why?"

"Let me answer your question with another question: why don't you accept every man's advances?"

"Because I'm not sure I can trust them."

"Well, there you go."

"But therapists are supposed to help you."

"Boyfriends are supposed to help you, aren't they?"

She chuckled when I said that.

"Okay, you got me. But there seems to be more to this. Don't rationalize your way out of this. Why are you against therapy personally?"

I didn't want to answer that, but since she was a stranger, there was little weight to what I was saying to her. So I thought I might as well confide.

"Well, in truth, I don't think there's another person on this planet who could understand who I am. There was a person, but she's long gone now."

"Aww, lost love huh?"

"You could say that. I know it's stupid to reminisce about someone so long ago. I know I should forget about her. But I can't. No matter how hard I try. But she wasn't like anyone else. I connected with her like no one else I've ever . . ."

Rebecca remarked, "Oh please, I bet you barely know anything about her."

"What?"

"I bet any woman who is nice to you is a savior in your eyes."

"That's not true."

She remarked again, "Oh, then tell me a little about her."

"Well, she had a passion for film, like I do. We would always discuss movies and analyze them."

"Okay, what else?"

"Well . . ."

"Tell me about her family, her struggles, what really matters to her."

I was silent, reflecting on the little knowledge I had about Rachel.

"You know nothing, as I thought. You make judgments about others based on what you think rather than what it is. I bet you barely know anything about your two friends you have with you."

"No, I don't. I cannot know everything. But that doesn't matter. Maddy and Lauro have always been kind to me. They sat by me at lunch, when no one else wanted to. Maddy and I discuss literature, and do deep dives into it. Lauro used his own cash in a misplaced effort so I could step out. They aren't perfect, but they're all I have. You know nothing about me, but you've decided to have a conversation with me for this long."

Rebecca laughed. "Whatever you say. But I'll bet you'll soon find out if they are as good friends as you think they are."

There was a long silence. Now was probably the time to ask for her phone number. But I lacked the power to do so. I was tired of debating and reflecting, and I just wanted to go home.

I got out of the booth, but before I walked away, Rebecca said, "Hey, maybe I'll see you around. I like to hang around here."

"Maybe so, and no one would have to pay you."

She laughed and got out of the booth as well. She went into her purse and grabbed the $50, handing it back to me.

"The time was priceless," and she walked away.

I couldn't agree more. Maddy and Lauro actually walked up to me. Lauro, as usual, was the first to jump in.

"So, did you ask her for her number?"

"No."

"No? You have a lot to learn, my friend."

Maddy, Lauro, and I walked out of the bar and they resumed their gossip. It was a shame, because I connected with them more than I ever had before. I saw another side of them. And despite Maddy's claim, these moments gradually decreased. As the months passed, Maddy, Lauro, and I began to see each other less and less. Without the convenience of school, the effort to put forth was too much for them. They often ignored my texts or calls for days on end before responding. It felt like I was an outsider on the precipice of the world they lived in. As time passed, I realized they weren't really my friends. I interacted with them at school, sure. But true friendship should go beyond mere interaction, shouldn't it?

We never matched the heart-to-heart that we shared on this night. Despite their kindness in school, they still were distant as friends as they were then. I would occasionally go to the bar in hopes of seeing Rebecca, but she never appeared. She said she'd "see me around." But out of all the nights I went there, no matter how many times I switched around the days or hours, I never saw her again. She too vanished with the wind. The night was like a bright light amidst a wave of darkness. But the light began to dwindle as time passed.

THE CATCHER IN THE RYE

I'd been reading a book. I found solace in it. It reignited my dwindling interest in life. Its grip on me was so strong that I hesitated to put it down, even when my insincere and phony existence beckoned back to me. Like Holden Caufield, I saw my life mirrored in his words. He comprehended the bewildering and flawed nature of human behavior. It was disheartening that my current companion existed only within the pages of fiction, but I related to it more than the shallow encounters I encountered every day. It was difficult to articulate my thoughts precisely. I couldn't clarify what I meant. And if I could, I'm not sure I would.

I needed something to divert my mind from the troubles that plagued me. So I lay in my bed in my modest new apartment, engrossed in continuous reading. I was a college freshman now, and reading was one of the only ways I could take my mind off my misfortunes. Occasionally, the fatigue of reading would set in, prompting me to wander around the small living space to rejuvenate my mind and body. My dad helped pay for my one-year lease. Though my apartment was no more than 500 square feet, it was sufficient for me. I had learned to make do with less.

However, there was one redeeming feature that compensated for the limited space—it offered an extraordinary view of the city. Situated on the highest floor of the building, which itself stood on elevated ground in the northern part of the city, my apartment provided a breathtaking vantage point. Every day as I peered out my window, I beheld a world seen through a lens unique to me. And now the time had come for my cherished daily ritual. I would venture on my veranda and witness the sunset. It was a magnificent sight, one that I relished each day. The slow descent of the dark red sun on the horizon filled me with a sense of fulfillment, surpassing any social interaction. I ironically dubbed it "Waterloo Sunset," as it evoked a feeling of empowerment rather than defeat as it drew to a close. Skyscrapers, the nearby mountains, and the world around me surged in my sight. At that moment my life was on pause, while everybody around me advanced. I always made time for it, shutting out all other concerns, just to immerse myself in the serenity it offered. Waterloo Sunset put me in paradise.

While lost in my reverie, blocking out the white noise, I wondered what Mom would think of the sunset. Then that thought disrupted my concentration of the sun's descent, and I stormed back inside to divert my mind elsewhere. But I found myself unable to focus, no matter the activity I engaged in. I was plunged in a state of torment that seemed to be thrust upon me by fate. The weight of my thoughts pressed against my chest.

As each passing person suggested to me, the allure of therapy tempted me every day. Yet, as a storm of conflicting thoughts raged within me, I still maintained that putting my life in someone else's hands was not the answer. I had spent years building shields, protecting myself from the disappointments of the world. The thought of someone breaking down those barriers ignited a fire within me. Amidst the chaos, the solace of the sunset and other activities brought fleeting moments of respite that whispered of my own strength and resilience.

Just then my cell phone rang from my desk. Glancing at the caller ID, I noticed it was Lauro. Presently, I had no desire to chew the fat or engage in idle conversation, so I let it ring. After a minute, the ringing ceased, and I noticed Lauro left a voicemail. Since I couldn't concentrate on anything else, I picked up the phone and listened to the voicemail out of curiosity.

"Hey Robbie, . . . Look, I don't want to come off as overbearing, but you haven't been responding to me and Maddy's texts or calls. We're really worried about you. . . . I don't know what else to say, but I'm sorry your dad died. When we had lunch together, you looked really sad, I could tell something was bothering you. I'm sorry if I pressed you, but once you blurted out that your dad died, you stormed off. It got us both really worried. I mean you lost your mom already; now you lose your dad while you're a college freshman. It just can take a heavy toll on your mental health. . . . Anyway, we're here to help you, Robbie. You can talk to us."

But I couldn't, could I? I was trying not to dwell on it. Trying and failing, like every other memory. Couldn't they understand that? Recollecting the past did me no good; it only halted the wheels of life. Yet they seemed oblivious to that fact. When I attempted to engage in a conversation, it rarely delved into intellectual topics. Instead, they reveled in gossip, always ready to critique and question the "mental health" of others. I hesitated to share anything with them, fearing their repulsion. While I wasn't above criticizing others, I refused to make it the essence of my existence.

Strangely enough, the conversations I overheard in my classes mirrored those of Lauro and Maddy. When I looked at the world, I struggled to find anything genuinely appealing. People appeared empty, devoid of original thought, mere cogs in a relentless wheel. Occasionally, Maddy engaged in conversations about Orwell, Wilde, or other authors I read, though it often veered into critiques of the racism, sexism, and lack of representation in the works. She was unable to analyze the art, and focused more on aspects that weren't part of the art. Still, I endured it, grateful for the opportunity to discuss something beyond the "craziness" of others. As for Lauro, his admiration for me and our enjoyable banter made him a comforting presence. So they were good to me when I saw them. But I seldomly saw them. They claimed to have little time for me, yet spent their days together. It irked me, but I tolerated it because I appreciated their company. I just wished I could be myself around them.

I intended to avoid further troubling thoughts, and I noticed the dark night sky outside my window. I had homework to finish for class, and needed some sleep. Fortunately, the homework involved reading the book I was just perusing, as I only had one class the next day. I settled into bed, picked up the book, and immersed myself in its pages, determined to regain my focus. After a few hours, I reached the assigned chapter and drifted off to sleep.

After a restful night, I arrived at my classroom, eager to discuss the brilliant nuances I had discovered within the book's lines. As I took my seat, the minutes passed, more and more people began to come in and sit down till the class was filled. The last to enter was our professor, Mr. Malcolm Clay, wearing his customary three-piece suit. He wore narrow white glasses, and possessed short black hair, apparently imitating another famous Malcolm. He prepared for class, and it was time for him to begin his sermon.

Surprisingly, he seemed more reserved than usual. "Good morning, class. I hope you all completed the assigned reading and have been introduced to Holden Caulfield. So, what are your initial thoughts?"

As soon as he spoke those words, dozens of hands shot up in the air. Mr. Clay smiled and randomly selected one to speak.

"I hated this guy. Basically all he does is whine about his problems, nothing at all what an enlightened protagonist should do."

After that remark, Mr. Clay began calling on everyone else in the class, each person sharing a corresponding opinion.

"If you're a rich and grumpy white man, this is a book for you."

"This guy is too blind to see how good he has it."

"This is worse than *Fight Club,* where privileged white men just moan about not having privileges."

These responses were not unpredictable, and Mr. Clay readied himself to launch into one of his impassioned monologues. He recited his words with the fervor of a Shakespearean actor, but it was evident he didn't truly engage with the ideas he presented. Had he done so, he might have realized that brevity is the soul of wit.

"Yes, as I'm sure all of you have noticed, this book raises serious issues in regard to racism and sexism. The protagonist, a privileged white boy attending a prestigious preparatory school, criticizes the behavior of those around him, shouting internally with all his might. He revels in his white privilege, oblivious to the mistreatment faced by those around him. This book serves as a stark reminder of how far we've come as a society and how much further we must strive!"

As the banal aphorism left his lips, applause erupted from the class. But all I did was just facepalm. How had this man received a teaching position? Instead of facilitating discussion and considering diverse perspectives, he simply asserted his own viewpoints, and the class blindly agreed. A teacher was supposed to teach you how to think, not what to think. I sighed, realizing that I was stuck in a classroom where the English professor remained unread and uninterested in fostering intellectual growth.

For the next hour, we meticulously dissected passages, focusing exclusively on the so-called "problematic" aspects of the novel. The classroom transformed into a chaotic scene, with various voices clashing, and Mr. Clay smiling and nodding like a self-satisfied Polonius after delivering a speech to Hamlet.

Mr. Clay noticed my disinterest and asked for some participation, his voice dripping with false enthusiasm,

"So Mr. Shelby, what are your thoughts on this passage?"

"Oh, nothing really. You've clearly analyzed the line with much better care than I could."

Mr. Clay seemed to register my sarcasm, but perhaps his throat was parched from all his proclamations, as he didn't launch into his usual attack. Maybe I should have taken a stand, boldly declaring that the book was not what they claimed it to be. But I lacked their fervor, their zealous determination to make their voices heard. Thankfully, the class soon ended, and I made my way home, fuming over the fact that I had to endure such a class every week with an uninspiring English professor. But then I remembered a wise maxim: "He who can, does; he who cannot, teaches."

The chaotic classroom discussion got me contemplating the book as a whole. I wasn't blind; I realized that Holden was written as an unreliable narrator. Virtually every single page was filled with his laments, and the colloquial teenage slang, popular during the time, was used to capture the essence of youth. However, it would be an unintelligent simplification to merely point fingers at Holden and brand him a wicked character. Many of his insights about society and its inhabitants were accurate, and he was far from brainless. Holden himself endured constant mistreatment throughout the novel, from being isolated from his family, to wandering aimlessly through the city for days, and even being physically assaulted. He saw society from a perspective others failed to grasp. Far from a privileged man, he carried the burdens of a teenager growing up in the '50s, burdened with more struggles and responsibilities than their twenty-first-century counterparts. This is what made the book so captivating—a man grappling with the weight of societal hypocrisies as he struggles to navigate the path to adulthood. Naturally, he made questionable decisions, as that is the very essence of humanity. An unreliable narrator, despite flaws, can still offer profound insights about society.

As I walked through the door of my apartment, I sought solace near a window, where I could watch my Waterloo Sunset. The beauty of the moment provided a temporary escape. However, the events of the day continued to creep into my thoughts, nagging at my mind. It reminded me of the countless times I had been unable to share my true thoughts, of how no one seemed interested in understanding who I truly was or what I believed. I carried the weight of my thoughts alone, putting on a brave face and pretending to be content. But there were moments when the weight became too much, when the cracks in my soul deepened and I felt as though I couldn't go on.

After a few minutes of contemplation, I rose from my seat and walked towards the closet in my bedroom. On the highest shelf, tucked away in a shoebox, lay a double-action revolver. Its dark frame and handle seemed to beckon to me, as if by wielding it I could tap into the very essence of the world around me. My dad had given it to me when I moved into my own apartment, a precautionary measure to protect myself from threats. I picked it up, feeling its weight in my hands, and returned to my spot by the window, just as the sun began its descent.

Thoughts of ending my own life occasionally plagued my mind. Though I tried to push them aside, they would resurface, lingering throughout the day. Feelings of loneliness and isolation would build, and I struggled to smile and put on a happy face. Sometimes, the idea of jumping from a tall building or falling from a towering flight of stairs seemed more appealing than living a joyless, parentless existence. I wondered if anyone would notice or care enough to catch me if I took the plunge. But more often than not, these thoughts emerged in the darkest hours of the night, robbing me of precious sleep. And I knew that if I were to share these feelings, I would become just another object of ridicule in Maddy and Lauro's conversations, another freak to be deplored.

Yet the weight of these persistent thoughts, though undoubtedly burdensome, strangely began to wane over time. With the amount of trauma I had experienced, despair was not surprising. Yet the sadness it brought couldn't sustain its grip on me, and I found myself able to ignore it. Even as I held the gun to my face, locked and loaded, safety off, ready to end it all, I couldn't bring myself to pull the trigger. The lack of willpower to take my own life stemmed from the realization that if I did, everything that was said or not said about me would be true. They would have been justified in avoiding me, as I could have caused them harm. That wasn't the legacy I wanted to leave behind. My driving force became the desire to prove them wrong and attain the power of which I had been unjustly deprived.

But the strongest motivation came from knowing that it wasn't what my mom wanted. She had fought tirelessly to catch me when I fell, and I couldn't throw that effort away. However, with each slip, each time she tried to free me from my cynical view of the world, a piece of her heart was lost. Eventually, she couldn't catch me anymore and all her heart vanished.

She had a strong heart, and she tried to give it to me in many ways, but it was all in vain. She spent all her time teaching me vocabulary that I could have learned myself. And for what? I found myself wishing that I had never known her! I just wanted something, anything, to stop the thought of missing her. Can you hear me, Mom? I don't want to deal with this anymore! I wish I could feel your love rather than your tears. Instead of feeling comforted by memories of you, you only brought pain. And I didn't even desire to dwell upon what happened to Dad. I couldn't even bring myself to process it. These thoughts haunted me relentlessly. These thoughts just came again and again. You were making my heart troubled; you were making me feel afraid.

I yearned for a companion who understood me, someone who could help take away the pain, like Rachel did—my Spanish class companion with whom I could actually communicate. The thought of her reminded me of the physical and emotional distance that now separated us. As the years continued to pass, I'd often wonder where she was, what she was doing, or who she was with. I attempted to stop checking her social media pages, but I lacked the power to relinquish the urge completely. The loss of that genuine connection was almost as harmful as the loss of my mom. The memories of my mom, since I was so young, weren't as clear and began to fade. Their absence brought pain, but the absence of connection brought nearly the same amount of pain. Rachel had left such a distinct impression that the loss of her refused to wane. I wished she would show up at my doorstep, willing to catch me when I fell. These moments of reflection momentarily made me powerless, although the sunset helped me sustain a semblance of power.

Then I heard a knock on the door. Realizing I had been shedding tears, I quickly wiped them away. That lasted longer than usual but I found the strength to push those thoughts aside once again. I returned the gun to its shoebox and placed it back in the closet. Peering through the peephole, I recognized who stood outside. I felt the urge to share the experience I had just gone through, but deep down I knew she would never understand. I opened the door, and greeted my guest.

"Hey, Maddy."

"Hey Robbie! Can I come in?"

No.

"Hell no . . . just kidding, of course."

She walked in and started chewing the fat, "How's it going?"

I feel like death, so nothing new.

"Nothing new, how are you?"

"Nothing new . . . or . . . .well . . . me and Lauro are worried about you."

"Look, you didn't have to come over here. I appreciate the concern, but it's not like I'm holding a gun to my head."

Maddy stared at me, a look of doubt in her eyes. After a few seconds, she gently ran her finger along my cheek, wiping away all the tears I couldn't feel. I closed my eyes for a brief moment and let out a sigh.

But before I could gather my thoughts, Maddy interjected, "You missed a spot."

I remained silent, unable to conjure up any wise words. Soon enough, I walked away from her and returned my gaze to the fading sunset. Suddenly, a voice from behind echoed words that distracted me from my view of the world.

"Look, Robbie . . . have you ever considered therapy?"

Rage began to boil within me as I clenched my fists.

"Why? Do you think a freak like me desperately requires it?"

She walked to my side and said, "There's nothing to be ashamed of Robbie. Nowadays, everybody goes to therapy. I have a therapist, Lauro has a therapist. Therapy is a place where broken people have a chance to heal. As a matter of fact, I can recommend you to our psychiatrist. His name's Doctor Robert Wolfe. He's a great guy and really improved our lives. I think you can learn a lot from the strength he's given both of us."

"So I'm broken? Is that what you and Lauro love to gossip about behind my back? This isn't about helping me; this is about turning me into everyone else."

She stepped forcefully in front of me, breaking my view of Waterloo Sunset.

"No! . . . Look Robbie, I'm just really concerned about you. All you do is just sit in here all day, only occasionally leaving your sanctuary to hang out with us. I know you prefer to be by yourself, but the outside world isn't so bad. You just gotta give it a chance. You gotta give therapy a chance. I think you can really benefit from it. . . . You already lost your mom, now you've lost your dad. I can't imagine what it's like to go through that without someone to talk to."

I had been trying to suppress the memories of what happened to my dad, but her mention of him stirred up profound sadness within me. Unable to find the words, I simply looked down, lost in my thoughts.

"What happened to him, Robbie?"

I looked up, my voice filled with a mix of sadness and anger,

"My dad used to work for a construction company. One of his coworkers, Packer, held a grudge against him. They got into a fight on their last day, and my dad won. Packer wrote a note and left it in his house, saying how angry he was at the world. He was filled with anger, and saw my dad as the embodiment of all his problems. He believed my dad was the biggest racist he ever met. Packer tailed my dad home before they fought, as my dad loved to irritate him. He planned to murder him, but for some reason, held it off for years. Maybe he didn't possess enough willpower. But his desire eventually grew, and at around midnight, Packer broke into my dad's house, shooting open a window. However, my dad was prepared. He had a shotgun hidden under his bed. He heard the commotion and grabbed the shotgun, confronting Packer near the front door. My dad shot him, but Packer still had enough life in him to shoot my dad in the heart. Despite his injury, my dad fired another shot, taking Packer's life. By the time the police arrived, it was too late. My dad bled out with a hole in his heart."

Maddy hugged me immediately, tears streaming down her face. I allowed the hug, but my focus remained on the sunset behind her.

"That's so awful, Robbie. . . . I'm so sorry . . . You should have told us sooner. . . . You've just been keeping that inside you for these past few months. No one should have to do that . . . . That's what made Packer do that, and I wouldn't want you to . . ."

She stopped after uttering those words. I pulled away from her abruptly.

"What are you implying?"

"I just don't want you to do something rash, that's all."

"How can you say that? How can you compare me to him? Packer couldn't control his anger, he had no outlet. Here, I have everything I need. I can read, watch TV, play video games, and watch the sunset; as long as I am here, I am in paradise. Any momentary despair eventually subsides, even if it feels ceaseless."

"What about people, Robbie? You can't live your life in isolation. You need to interact with others to grow as a person. People can help alleviate the stress you feel. Therapy can help you heal."

"No, I don't need to force unnecessary stress on myself. I don't need a doctor repeating in my ear how great I have it. I don't need to acquire more superficial friendships. I have enough fake friends as it is."

Maddy stood in silence when I said that, but I added onto my reply. "I barely see you guys anyway, and I know it'll be the same with whomever I attempt to befriend. But you think I haven't tried to make friends with people? You think I want to be up here all alone watching a sunset? No, I've just learned to appreciate it. It's more fulfilling than interacting with any more phonies. Whenever I ask to see someone, they always say they're busy. But no one is ever too busy for their friends. Yet it's a refrain I hear whenever I try to connect with someone. They keep saying how much they miss me without making any effort to see me. Pretty soon, enough time has passed that they move on with their life, and disappear from mine. But you should be very familiar with this, because you and Lauro barely make an effort to see me anymore. Soon enough, you and Lauro will be gone like the wind.

"And you might blame me. Miss Blackwell might say, 'People shouldn't be forced into toxic interactions with others. You need to reevaluate your interactions with others and don't make them feel excluded.' But I have considered that, and have attempted multiple ways in trying to befriend others. I have tried multiple ways in trying to turn the big wheels, to be like everybody else. But that has always resulted in the same outcome, me lying on the floor in agony alone. I shouldn't have to make an extraordinary effort to change who I am just to please others. If others are always going to view me as the problem, then I won't bother dealing with it. Maybe I'm not the problem. I refuse to compromise who I am just for the sake of others, as I know they wouldn't do the same for me. And I know you wouldn't do it either.

"I inhabit an imperfect institution with idiotic itches, inclination with no inspiration, idealized inferiority, and no intellectual invigoration." Wilde would be proud that I sounded that out loud, without any help from a crowd.

I unleashed all my pent-up emotions, not considering the consequences of my words. Maddy looked distressed, and I contained a hint of regret, but I knew I needed to express myself. After a few seconds of silence, Maddy finally spoke.

"Was there a funeral?"

"Funerals are for those who have family or friends. My dad didn't have friends, and I am his only family. I have neither."

My words struck a heavy blow, and I saw Maddy shed a tear when she barged out of the room. Regret surged inside me, but I remained resolute in my decision. I convinced myself that I didn't need the company of fake friends. I had seen this before, a fleeting concern to check on me, followed by an expectation to move on as if nothing had happened. I wanted to break free from this cycle.

But regret continued to simmer within me, boiling my blood. I needed a distraction, something to divert my mind, but my sunset was burned out, and darkness engulfed me. I turned on a light and found myself drawn to the closet. As I opened it, I noticed another small cardboard box, nestled near my shoebox. It was a relic from the time when I had to clear out my father's house after his passing. Most of his belongings were sold or discarded, but I had kept this box. Curiosity compelled me to place it on the living room table, and from inside I picked out my mother's diary.

Until that moment, I had never felt the desire to read it. But now it seemed like the perfect time to unburden myself from another weight on my mind. For hours I immersed myself in the manuscript, a tearful journey through my mother's deepest struggles. Commenting on every page would be unnecessary, as the raw emotions poured onto the paper were profoundly saddening. The diary revealed my mom's relentless quest for perfection and her battle with identity. Witnessing my parent in such a vulnerable state shattered my perception. Growing up, our parents are the spectacles through which we view the world. Their actions, even if unconventional, seem normal. But now, seeing my mother's fragility, I began to question my own understanding. Moreover, after reading for so long, I ran into passages that made me squirm in my seat.

I received Robbie's End of the Year Literacy Evaluation today, along with a meeting with one of the teachers for his 1st grade class. She said that he has wonderful fluency, but very low comprehension of his fluency levels; he struggles with understanding directions and tasks, and that he can't write a summary because he can't filter the important material from the unnecessary facts. She said he worked with a star tutor, but she recommended I transfer him out of the private school because of how low his scores are. I didn't listen, I know my boy is perfect, he just needs encouragement.

I worry that my boy will be bullied and not fit in with the other kids at school. So I started tutoring him. I make him read the dictionary and write out words in sentences every day. It's hard for him to learn; he frequently wanders off task and shows no interest in learning. One day he repeatedly asked me the time in a session, even when there was a normal clock on the wall near him. So I spent a day trying to teach him how to tell time, and he still struggles with it. It makes me wonder if Robbie will ever grow in intelligence, if he'll even be able to read a book on his own. But I keep on trying. It's been two years since my cancer diagnosis, and I just couldn't take it anymore, I had to tell him. But he couldn't understand. After explaining it in multiple ways, even flat out telling him that I will die, he couldn't process the information. He just stood there and shrugged it off, eventually going back to idling around. After I told him that, I just couldn't tutor him any longer that day, and sent him to bed. While he slept sound asleep, I stayed awake in the hours of the night, wondering what will become of my son.

Stunned, I dropped the manuscript in my hand and stood up in my seat. That's wasn't possible. How did I not remember that at all? If I had been such an academic failure, how was I able to improve and develop a love for reading? But then doubt crept in. What if it was true? Perhaps I cherished reading so deeply because it was a skill I had to work hard to acquire. If that were the case, then everything I believed about myself was a lie. I wasn't a polymath. I wasn't even average. I was less than an idiot. Her heart-wrenching admissions of failure as a parent stared back at me. The weight of her self-blame crushed me, as if I carried her burden with me. It shattered my heart. I had been blind to the reality of my own limitations. I didn't look at the world as well as I thought. It rendered me so powerless that it made me look to anything to regain that power.

After a few minutes of shock, a single thought consumed my mind: I had to call Maddy. It was close to midnight, and the odds of her still being awake were slim, but I took the chance. After several rings, she finally answered.

"Hello?" Maddy's voice sounded weary.

"Maddy! I'm so sorry for my words today. I think I've come to realize that I've misunderstood so many things in my life, including our friendship. You and Lauro have been there for me, and I haven't acknowledged that. I'm just truly sorry for berating you today, you nowhere near deserved that."

"No, Robbie. I've been thinking about what you said, and I must admit, me and Lauro haven't been around for you as well as we should have. We have considered that we do leave you out of our conversations and don't include you enough. Your words, though hurtful, held some truth and opened my eyes. But I want to make it up to you."

My voice shook as I confided in Maddy, sharing the depths of my remorse and vulnerability. She listened with unwavering compassion, her understanding a ray of light in a world full of darkness. The realization dawned on me that perhaps therapy could offer solace, a way to navigate the labyrinth of my own mind. The resistance within me began to break, replaced by a flicker of acceptance.

"That's kind of you to say, but I truly acknowledge I was in the wrong. My eyes have been opened . . . Maddy, please help get me in touch with Doctor Robert. I've come to realize that I need therapy now more than ever. And Maddy, you recommended him to me, even when I resisted.

You knew my mental state better than I. You fought for me, and even though it pained me, I'm grateful. Because the moment you walked out that door, I felt an overwhelming sense of longing for you. I miss so many people now. I wish I could express how much I miss them. I wish I could tell them anything . . . I could tell anybody anything."

PART 2:
A CLOCKWORK ORANGE

8.

BRAVE NEW WORLD

Pain was a transfixing trepidation. A few weeks earlier, I had confided in Maddy about my interest in seeking therapy. That perhaps I wasn't living my life to its full potential. That perhaps I was wrong. *Perhaps.* That word gnawed at my brain, like an insidious drug that eroded my cognizance and autonomy. The pain that a single word could wield over us was astonishing.

Now, seated in Doctor Robert's waiting room, my thoughts consumed me. The room was sterile, painted entirely in white. The starkness unsettled me, sending a shiver down my spine. It looked like the very essence of hope had been sucked out of the room, leaving a void that permeated the air. Amidst the plain white table, a dozen white chairs lined in the periphery. Even the receptionist's desk was an expanse of snowy white. Everything was so clinical, it intensified my unease, leaving me unable to focus on anything but my swirling thoughts. Doubts crept in like unwelcome guests. Perhaps this Doctor Robert wasn't who he claimed to be. Perhaps.

Initially, I had been so willing to shed my old life, to embrace change without hesitation. But now, standing on the precipice of the unknown, second thoughts flooded my mind, not to mention third, fourth, and fifth thoughts. The doubts multiplied, like an incessant chorus of questions.

Just as the claustrophobia threatened to engulf me, the receptionist called my name from her desk. She was still sitting down and kept her eyes on her computer as I walked towards her. Her name plaque read "Ashley Lawson." Her eyes finally met mine. And I must say, she really cut a dash.

Adorned with narrow-rimmed black glasses, her mesmerizing blue eyes captivated me. Her flawless complexion complemented her long, relaxed black hair. She wore a simple white dress shirt, a few buttons undone, revealing . . . well, let's just say her cleavage created a chasm that rivaled the Grand Canyon. Completing her ensemble were black heels and a tight skirt that hugged her shapely figure, accentuating her . . . curves. It appeared that the dress code at Doctor Robert's office was quite lax, which begged the question of why she chose to dress this way. The tendrils of doubt tightened their grip on me once more.

"Like what you see?"

Great. How can I word my way out of this?

"Your choice of clothing reveals much of your inner character."

"Thank you!"

What? She actually bought that? That must be the smoothest thing I ever said to a woman. Perhaps my flirtation skills were improving. She stood up.

"The doctor is ready to see you now. Follow me."

She said this with her back turned toward me. Her stride spoke volumes about her physical presence, and it was difficult to resist the temptation to ogle. I found myself captivated by her, and as I glanced up, she tilted her head slightly, acknowledging my fleeting glance. A smile graced her lips. The drug of uncertainty coursed through my veins, but I managed to maintain composure.

The hallway, like the waiting room, was devoid of color, painted in plain white. We walked towards a black door with white lettering that read, "Doctor Robert." The distance was short, and my apprehension continued to mount. Once I arrived at the door, Ms. Lawson uttered, "Enjoy your session," then put her hand on my shoulder and blew me an air kiss. I was more stunned than gratified, yet she strutted away. I could have jokingly wolf-whistled, but I had to remember that I was in therapy now and shouldn't be making judgments. I needed to be open to opportunities for change. I realized that it was odd for me to see myself through the door; that's something a receptionist usually does, but perhaps the action of opening a door would have made her skirt tear.

Anger began to simmer within me, a response to the peculiar signs that seemed to urge me to be on guard. I found myself in a brave new world, and I had to summon the courage to make decisions for what lay ahead. However, I couldn't help but find humanity no more beautiful than before.

Yet I recalled the countless signs I had been misinterpreting in my life, a consequence of the extensive trauma I endured. I now perceived that these signs were likely illusions, figments of my damaged psyche, which a therapist could help me unravel. I ignored any rational criticism of what was exposed to me, and tried to keep an open mind. As Maddy, Lauro, and countless others advised, I needed to give therapy a chance. I stood before the door, ready to turn the handle and step inside. However, a small voice within warned me to tread cautiously.

A whimsical thought crossed my mind as I imagined myself kicking the door open like "Rowdy" Roddy Piper, as if it would reveal the doctor to be an alien in disguise. Perhaps he possessed a death ray, slowly disintegrating his unsuspecting patients. Or perhaps he hailed from Uranus, a lover of probing human subjects, hence the fondness for his human secretary. Or worse, he could be a covert alien agent, plotting to amass a fortune and secure a peaceful existence for his entire race. I laughed out loud at these preposterous possibilities. Surely, a person of such societal importance couldn't be an alien in disguise.

I turned the doorknob and entered the room, but there was no warm welcome or red carpet. Instead, I found a man engrossed in a book, his face hidden behind its cover. His room stood in stark contrast to the rest of the office; everything was painted black, from the bookcase to the chair to the desk. Even his attire matched the darkness of the room, with a black dress shirt and pants. Curiosity piqued, I took a seat in the chair he gestured towards, relieved that this room at least offered some variation in aesthetics. Glancing around, I noticed a doctorate degree hanging on the wall, a photograph of a family (that of a boy, mother, and father), and an unexpected painting: van Gogh's *Prisoners Exercising,* a depiction of confined individuals walking aimlessly in a circle. The image reminded me of Stanley Kubrick's film *A Clockwork Orange.* Unfortunately, the sight of that painting made the intensity of the drug at an all-time high. I pondered if I would be little Alex, eventually being subjected to the Ludovico Technique, my volition violated.

As I sat in silence, I realized the man was reading *The House of God.* The irony struck me, and I wondered if he understood the implications of the laws of The House of God. Finally, he closed the book, leaned back in his chair, and focused his gaze on me. He seemed amiable, his smile radiating a warmth that caught me off-guard.

His appearance hardly resembled that of a traditional doctor. He possessed a well-built physique, his clothes clinging tightly, while his short black hair and symmetrical face appeared like those of a model. I squirmed a bit inside, as if I were looking in a mirror, seeing something of myself reflected in him. In another life, perhaps we could have been the same person.

He remained silent. The peculiarities of this place had worn my patience thin, and I couldn't resist making a quip.

"You know, for a psychiatrist you're not doing a great job. I thought you're supposed to show some care and concern for your patients, not bury yourself in a book like you encountered your first porn magazine."

He smirked at my comment, so I just continued. "Speaking of which, maybe you should have chosen a career in real estate. Your room designs are truly one of a kind. Walking through an all-white waiting room and hallway, only to end up in an all-black room really gets me in the mood. Are you hiding your supervillain costume somewhere here?"

He laughed out loud, prompting me to finish with one last killer line.

"You must also possess some mind control. There's no way any woman would want to work in such a workplace, let alone a woman that attractive. And why do you make her dress like she's preparing for a porn casting? Is it because your testosterone is so high that you sleep with your secretary just to get through the day?"

His laughter eventually subsided, and he fell silent. Frustrated, I demanded a response.

"Answer me! Say something!"

"I have a name."

"What?"

"I have a name. My name is Doctor Robert Wolfe, but you can call me Doctor Robert. Can you do that?

"What?"

"Can you say the following phrase: 'Hello, Doctor Robert'?"

Begrudgingly, I did as he asked. "Hel-lo, Doc-tor Rob-ert."

While smirking he replied, "Good. Do you know why I made you say that?"

"No, but I bet you'll monologue why."

"It's because I am a human being, just like you. I have my own strengths, weaknesses, past, and future, just like you. In many ways, we are the same, we are all the same. While my expertise lies in psychiatry, I have been trained to provide therapy to patients. I possess knowledge that can improve your life, relationships, and decision-making. You can see proof of my expertise on that wall, where my doctorate degree hangs. I am dedicated to your personal growth and satisfaction, as long as you follow my guidance. However, if this doesn't interest you, you're free to walk out that door at any time; I won't judge you. But since you sought me out, I'm willing to bet that you aren't entirely fulfilled with your life, are you?"

After a brief pause, I reluctantly stated, "No, I am not."

This prompted Doctor Robert to grab a black clipboard and a pen, ready to write.

"So . . . to whom do I have the pleasure of speaking?"

"Robbie . . . .Robbie Shelby."

"Robbie, from your remarks I can tell that you lack confidence in my abilities as a doctor. Is this a fair assumption?"

"More than fair."

"Why do you feel such distrust towards me?"

"Some studies show that medical malpractice is the third leading cause of death in the United States. Now, that's for all doctors. For psychiatrists specifically, a majority of them will prescribe patients medication even when they think it's unnecessary. The medications alter the chemicals in the brain and can cause side effects such as internal bleeding, nausea, fatigue, insomnia, and so much more. But psychiatrists often feel forced to provide medication as a quick solution to appease a patient's desires. Yet when I discuss these studies with others, they dismiss them. They claim that doctors are extensively educated and can be trusted with our health, as if the science is flawless.

"But let me ask you this: if we consider a standard practice like hand-washing before surgery, it's common sense, right? Well, that didn't become common practice until the 1800s, after a doctor dared to go against the grain, and was laughed at. He was ridiculed and deemed idiotic for suggesting something that wasn't accepted practice. As such, just because therapy is accepted doesn't mean it's necessarily an effective approach to improving patient health. I have no reason to believe that I will improve my well-being after leaving your sessions, and from what I've seen walking in here, you're not giving me any good reasons otherwise."

As the words spilled out of me, he sat there silently, his pen gliding across the paper. The sound seemed to echo in the room, a tangible symbol of his detachment from my concerns. When I finally finished, he continued to write, as if my words were merely a backdrop to his thoughts.

Then, with a small smirk on his face, he interrupted the stillness by picking up a book from his desk.

"Are you familiar with this book?" he asked, a hint of challenge in his voice.

"*The House of God*? Yes."

"What do you know about it?"

I responded. "It's a satire."

"Come now, I know you have more to say than that."

"Satire is an essential part of a functional society. It holds a mirror up to our flaws and shortcomings, reminding us that nothing is exempt from criticism. It permeates all forms of art, subtly blending into our culture over time, often unnoticed. The beauty of satire lies in its ability to challenge the status quo and provoke thought."

A small laugh escaped his lips, his eyes gleaming with amusement. He responded swiftly, his words carrying a different meaning,

"One could argue that satire allows us to see beyond ourselves. Solitary activities allow an individual to distance themselves from reality. But too much of it can prove too dangerous, inflating the ego of the uneducated, giving them a false sense of understanding. This particular book perpetuates a stigma against doctors. They are portrayed as half-witted, venereal schmucks whose patients are in better health when they are not being treated by them. While amusing, this is inaccurate on the many challenges and successes doctors have in caring for their patients. A good satire always touches the other side.

"Robbie, I can assure you you're not the first person to walk through that door to express distrust towards me or doctors in general, and you certainly won't be the last. And that's perfectly okay. I can't expect you to trust me simply because I ask. There is some evidence to suggest that doctors may not have a patient's best interest at heart. However, what I can promise you is this: see that degree hanging on the wall? It took me eight years of rigorous education to earn that degree. The college I attended was incredibly competitive, and missing just three classes meant failing the course. Those classes consisted of hours upon hours of lectures, and hours upon hours of homework about human behavior, its hardships, joys, and areas of improvement. Many of my patients come to me feeling unfulfilled by the world and searching for answers. Deep down, they are broken and disconnected from their best selves.

"Robbie, we've only just met, but that's not what I want for you. I want you to walk out of this room and navigate your life with ease. Am I asking you to compensate me? Yes I am, you got me. I have a monetary incentive, but that doesn't mean I can't care for my patients. Those studies you've mentioned are just a few widely publicized ones, with many inaccuracies, biases, and sample size problems. I've read them as well, and I'm not the only doctor who has reservations with them. I'm reading this book, right now, to better myself as a doctor, to see the other side. I desire to understand any distrust you have. I want to be the doctor who made you change your mind about doctors."

His words resonated within me, challenging my preconceived notions. I had never considered the perspective of doctors, the struggles they faced, the dedication they had to their profession. Once I started to listen to him, it was like he was singing me a song that I was waiting to hear.

But I was still biting my tongue. The signs I had noticed upon entering his office forced doubts to linger in my mind. I couldn't let go of my ambivalence, but I played along for now.

I remained silent after his last line, searching for the right words, trying to grasp my next thought. But the doctor's gaze locked onto mine, seemingly peering down into the deep recesses of my soul, unraveling the layers of my being with each consecutive stare.

Sensing my hesitation, he seamlessly transitioned into his next idea, ready to navigate the depths of my doubts.

"Still not sold, are you? That's alright. Tell me what's troubling you."

"It's just . . . all these puzzling things I noticed when I walked in your office. The waiting room, completely white—the chairs, the tables, even the hallway, all white. And this room, in stark contrast, is all black, even your attire. Your secretary, to put it bluntly, dresses like she wants to be boned by every patient's bone. Explain that to me."

He smiled, his gaze was unwavering,

"Robbie, rest assured that you are not the first person to ponder about the intricacies of human behavior. It's what makes each individual unique. But tell me Robbie, why do you think the secretary's attire and my office space are wrong?"

"What?"

"On what basis do you classify my office decorations as incorrect?"

"I . . . I don't know."

"Consider this. We have a cable television network dedicated entirely to home improvement and design: HGTV. Have you ever watched that channel? The architecture and design that clients desire for their homes can be just as unconventional as my office space. It is simply an expression of personal taste and comfort. As for my secretary, it is not my place to dictate her choice of clothing.

"Your first lesson is to reflect on how you perceive the world around you. People may make choices that you disagree with or find peculiar, such as architectural styles or clothing choices, but that doesn't make you superior to them. I want you to consider the reasons behind their decisions and avoid jumping to conclusions. From what you've just told me, there seems to be a disconnect between how you view the world and how the world views you. Recognizing this disconnect will help you maneuver through life with greater ease."

His words struck a chord within me, resounding with truth that I couldn't deny. His voice enveloped me in a calm, soothing embrace, his words flowing like a gentle stream that caressed my troubled thoughts. Yet even as I sat in contemplative silence, I couldn't fully embrace it. An underlying unease lingered from all the earlier signs. With a surge of determination, I rose from my chair, intending to leave. But his voice stopped me in my tracks.

"Robbie, I can sense your discomfort. It's not uncommon for patients to feel that way on their first day. It's part of the process. Confronting that discomfort is an essential part of therapy, enabling you to confront your inner demons. That being said, if you feel I'm not the right doctor for you, you're free to leave. I won't stop you. However, I promise to address any concern you may have and answer your questions with complete honesty. I want you to know that you couldn't be in safer hands."

His words hung in the air, and resonated within me. I surrendered to his persuasion, and slowly turned around, resumed my seat, and met his gaze again.

"You've convinced me, Doctor Robert. I'll take a step into your world."

Yet another smile graced his lips, reflecting a mix of satisfaction and anticipation. Before we continued our session, he imparted a piece of advice that stuck with me, soothing my restless nights.

"Remember Robbie, all people are equal. You may feel they're in a different domain, but I admire you taking a step outside your own world. It's a brave act that has brought solace to countless others, and I'm confident you'll find it equally rewarding."

9.

PRISONERS EXERCISING

Under a starry night sky, I sat on my veranda, captivated by its beauty. I had just witnessed my Waterloo Sunset, and decided to keep gazing at the sky, or more specifically, the stars. Their distant glow seemed to hold the secrets to eternity, illuminating the otherwise pitch-black night. Each star appeared as a bright entity, swirling with energy and power, casting its light upon the world below. I couldn't help but be entranced, my gaze shifting from one star to another, as if they were living beings, transmitting some of its potency to me.

As the night progressed, a faint light emerged over the city: the rising sun. Its arrival brought a new sense of power and awe, surpassing that of the stars. It dawned on me that I had spent the entire night lost in my stargazing, oblivious to the passing time and need for rest. It might sound foolish to be so absorbed in such a simple act, but it was a part of who I am. Was this why I was in therapy? No, I shouldn't be ashamed of embracing my own uniqueness, even if it meant being alone in my perception of the world. But I desired to meet someone who could see the night sky the way I see it.

As I sat in my car in the parking lot, contemplating my thoughts, I wondered what Doctor Robert would say. Would he understand the internal conflict I faced, choosing between embracing my true self or conforming to fit in? Uncertainty clouded my mind as I stepped out of the car and gazed up at the towering building before me. Its architecture blended seamlessly with the rest of the cityscape, but one window caught my attention. Behind it, a man looked down at me, smiling. Though this gesture evoked suspicion, I reminded myself not to jump to conclusions. Therapy was meant to help me find someone who understood me, someone who shared my perspective on the world. And this man, this doctor, could help me find that person.

Entering the building and making my way to the doctor's office, I approached Ms. Lawson's desk. With a friendly smile, she checked me in while engrossed in something on her computer screen, and I sat back down. Even though her appearance was revealing, I reminded myself, as Doctor Robert had taught me, not to judge others based on my own perceptions. Though I was still slightly staggered, I tried to learn to appreciate the idiosyncrasies and refrain from harsh judgments.

While I waited, Ms. Lawson's telephone rang, and after a brief conversation, she informed me that the doctor was ready to see me. As I approached her desk, she stood out of courtesy, but I replied.

"No need to get up, I can escort myself. And I can tell you're busy."

"Oh thank you!"

As she sat down, I noticed that she was drinking a glass of milk. And I just couldn't resist a playful quip.

"You're drinking milk? Isn't that something children drink?"

"Doctor Robert recommends that I drink milk for my health. But it's not just for children. Most people drink milk nowadays, like Robert's patients."

Oblivious to my sarcasm, her response came with a genuine smile—innocent and unbothered like a helpless little fledgling. She sounded like someone under a person's thumb, incapable of thinking for herself. In the past, such a reaction would have urged me to bolt out the door, consumed by fear. But due to the doctor's orders, I chose to brush it off and remain composed.

With measured steps, I approached the doctor's door—a somber entrance devoid of stars—and entered his dimly lit room. Once again, he was engrossed in a book, this time Anthony Burgess's *A Clockwork Orange*.

Seizing the opportunity to playfully disrupt his focus, I inserted my hand into the pages he was reading and slammed the book shut on his desk, demanding his attention.

"Your patient is here, and it would be nice if you gave him the attention he deserves."

Startled and leaning back in his chair, he seemed taken aback by my audacity. Undeterred, I claimed the seat in front of his desk, prompting him to respond.

"I see you haven't learned your lesson. Did it ever occur to you that I was absorbed in something important?"

"No, because you weren't really reading. I saw you outside the window. If you were really reading, you wouldn't have been shadowing my arrival. You feign reading to incorporate book ideas for our sessions. It's your therapeutic technique."

He clasped his hands together and straightened in his seat, considering my words.

"Well . . . .what's it going to be then, eh?" I playfully asked.

"You're partially correct. . . . What I want to talk about is the painting behind me."

I gazed behind him at the painting. As I noted before, it was a van Gogh called *Prisoners' Round*, more commonly known as *Prisoners Exercising*.

"So, what do you see, Robbie?"

"Prisoners walking around in a circle."

He replied, "Don't give me that. You have an appreciation for art. So please explain what symbolism you derive from this portrait."

"It's satirical."

"Go on."

I explained, "Prison is meant to rehabilitate individuals, yet the prisoners are forced to walk around in a circle, seemingly endlessly. There is no beginning, there is no end. It is an exercise of conforming them to society, turning their behavior to clockwork as obedient cogs in society's machine. One could make this critique on all forms of rehabilitation."

"Yes. Let's talk about that, free will, a touted but fallacious concept."

"A man who ceases to choose, ceases to be a man."

He countered, "Then you have been caught in a cultural trap. Society requires structure and order, and there will always be those who seek to disrupt the natural harmony of society. Take the novel *A Clockwork Orange*. It challenges us to sympathize with a murderer and a rapist, suggesting that attempting to change a person is hypocritical. However, society cannot function with individuals running amok, acting solely on their desires. But you're right, you can't just forcibly stretch their eyelids while pouring liquid into their eyes; that wouldn't be moral either. But we have to teach little boys like Alex that murder and rape aren't the right way either. So what is the compromise? Therapy. I am not taking away anyone's free will. I am merely showing a better way to find a person who you can connect to, to fit in."

"What is the better way exactly?"

"Robbie, as a student of neuroscience, I understand the intricacies of the human brain. We are fundamentally social beings, wired to connect with one another. Failure to do so is a failure at the level of the brain. It's not your fault, but therapy can help you understand yourself and your body, and ultimately help you find a way to fit in. It's about forging genuine connections and teaching individuals like you that there are alternative ways to navigate life without resorting to harmful actions."

I mulled over his words. Dr. Robert's insights resonated with my deepest desires—to find acceptance and belonging. It was what I craved, especially in the wake of my experience with Rachel. She was always on my mind, and I couldn't get her out of my head. Even last night, while staring at the cosmos, I wondered if she was looking at the same night sky and could see what I saw. She had left me feeling broken and abandoned, but I refused to believe her actions reflected something inherently wrong with me.

"Is that what you want, Robbie?"

Yes.

"No."

"Really? Do you actually believe that?" Doctor Robert asked.

"Yes. People shouldn't just abandon you or renounce others just because they're different, whether it be a brain disorder or something else. When you love someone, you can't just stop loving someone because things become difficult or challenging. People who truly love each other never give up on each other. . . . If people have difficulty loving me, that reflects problems with them, not me. It doesn't excuse them to vanish like the wind."

"Does it? That sounds like a personal example."

"Yes. Yes it is."

"Would you care to tell me what happened?"

And I told him. I told him everything that happened with Rachel. Our conversations, our jokes, our date, and her being gone like the wind. It felt liberating to finally open up about the painful experience I kept hidden for so long. It was refreshing. I never was comfortable explaining to anyone what happened, even to Maddy and Lauro. But with Doctor Robert, a sense of trust and understanding compelled me to share my perspective of the world.

As I poured out the story, he remained perfectly engaged. He maintained unwavering eye contact and offered me tissues when my emotions overflowed. Tears streamed down my face as I expressed my anguish, questioning how Rachel could have acted the way she did. He was engrossed and absorbed, always maintaining proper eye contact, and allowed me to let out all the emotions I had bottled up about her. That sadness had been bottling up over the years. When I started crying and he offered me tissues, I resisted at first, but I took them due to his insistence. I started spouting things like "How could she do this?" and "We were so close." Finally, after letting me recenter myself, he asked a question.

"Robbie, let me ask you something. Would you have considered Rachel a good friend when you knew her?"

"Yes. Absolutely. How could I not?"

"How do you know that?"

Confused, I asked, "What do you mean by how do I know? What are you implying?"

"Well, did she ever ask you to spend time with her?"

"Well, we always messaged each other at night."

"Did you two ever spend time together besides the date?"

"No."

"Rachel was a popular girl, sought after by many. This suggests her charisma extended beyond just you, hinting at the fact that many other people felt this way around her. As such, she likely was acting like herself. Or do you believe that she made you feel special specifically?"

"No."

"Finally, she had a boyfriend the whole time you knew her aside from one date, plus she had many other boyfriends that you saw right after she disestablished contact. With this information in mind, do you truly believe she felt the same way about you? Do you truly believe she loved you?"

"No."

As that last "no" escaped my lips, my heart sank. A part of me always knew this, but I clung to a glimmer of hope, refusing to acknowledge the painful reality.

"Doctor, how can a person who made me feel so happy just vanish from my life?"

"Was she vanishing, Robbie? Or was she just living her life? People come and go like the wind; it's just a part of life. And if people leave your life repeatedly, or if people don't want to be around you, it's a sign that something might be wrong with your brain. . . . It's a hard lesson, but you have to learn it. The first part of solving any problem is to accept it."

These lines of reasoning stunned me with how much sense they made. But Doctor Robert quickly added, "But she's not the only person who vanished from your life, was she?"

"No . . . I also lost my mom when I was twelve years old. . . . And I lost my dad not too long ago."

"I'm so sorry Robbie . . . I'm . . ."

"No, no you're not."

"What?"

"You're not sorry. You barely know me. . . . The worst part of losing my mom and dad was not losing them, but receiving no support after they died. All you and others have to say are banal platitudes that mean nothing."

"Well, what would you like me to say, Robbie?"

I briefly considered his words and replied, "That you don't know what to say."

"Okay. 'I don't know what to say.' Now how am I or others supposed to know this? How are we supposed to know the right words to say?"

I considered some more, and after a long silence, Doctor Robert explained, "I want you to consider that the people around might not have all the answers and may not be as strong as you think they are."

Then the hardest sentence I ever spoke came out of my mouth.

"I suppose you're right."

My voice held a tinge of dejection as I slumped in my seat, my gaze fixed on the floor. I felt like a failure.

"Now Robbie, there's nothing to be ashamed of. You're not going to like what I'm going to say next, but you'll need to hear it if you want to fit in."

I looked up at him.

"Robbie, I'm diagnosing you with autism."

"No, that's impossible . . . I can't be a freak."

"No Robbie, you misunderstand. You're not a freak. Your brain is just wired differently, which can make it challenging for you to fit in with others. Autistic people have difficulties with socialization, and perform repetitive solitary habits, which I'm afraid you have disclosed to me. I can say with almost certainty that you have it. You have a milder form of it, but you still have it."

My brain lurched. My entire life flashed before my eyes. All those years. All those years of me eating lunch alone. All those years of not being able to make friends. All those years of not finding someone who could see the world like I did, that was my fault, a problem with me, not others. I couldn't believe it.

"But it's not too late to change, Robbie. There are techniques you can learn to socialize with others, and I can prescribe you medication that can mitigate your autistic tendencies. Don't worry, with my guidance, you'll be just like everybody else. I'll have you running like clockwork."

"Do whatever you need to do, Doc. I just want to fit in. I want to see what others can see."

As I trudged away from the doctor's office, I struggled to find the strength to put one foot in front of the other. Ashley bid me goodbye, but I couldn't muster a response. I got into the elevator and pushed the button for the ground floor, plunging myself to the ground. My energy had been completely drained, leaving me lifeless. Thoughts swirled in my mind, blaming my brain disorder as the sole cause of my misfortunes. Would Rachel still be by my side if I weren't autistic? Would I have been a better son? What was I supposed to do now?

Suddenly, the elevator doors opened to reveal a man in a trench coat ready to step in. However, he paused when he saw me sitting on the floor, lost in my own thoughts. I paid him no attention, gazing off into space as he stared at me with his hands on his hips.

"Excuse me, this is just a guess, but I think there are better areas to sit, such as a chair, car seat, anywhere really, I don't care. As long as it doesn't impede people trying to use the elevator . . ."

I had no desire to respond. I simply wanted to sit there, powerless.

He cleared his throat loudly. "What are you? Autistic?"

I clenched my fists in rage, but picked myself up and exited the elevator. I slowly walked towards the exit, while the man entered the elevator. At the last moment, he stopped the elevator from closing and walked up behind me, gently touching me on the shoulder.

"I'm sorry, that was rude of me. My doctor advised me to control my anger to make others feel comfortable, you know, to fit in. Let's start over. My name is Vinnie. And yours?"

"Robbie. And I don't blame you for the quip. If I was you, I would have done the same in your position. Although your delivery needs work. It should be much drier to have the desired effect. And a man with such an atrocious trench coat shouldn't lecture me on decorum. Seriously, where did you get that thing? It looks like it came out of a poorly painted picture."

"Hahaha. I just sort of lost my temper; it comes out sometimes; I apologize again. And I'll have you know that this trench coat perfectly represents my personal style, I just couldn't resist wearing it despite how abnormal it is. I just wanted to be me, you know?"

I answered, "Hell, with that beard of yours, you'll always be ugly. So that trench coat is actually a good decision—it distracts from your ugliness."

"Hahaha. I like you . . . How about we get some drinks tonight?"

"I'm not old enough to drink."

"You wouldn't be the first. That just means I have to supply the drinks. Meet me at my apartment later tonight, and be prepared for your first hangover. I'm meeting with my doctor right now, and I'll be right over."

Before, I might have considered it a bad idea to meet a stranger in their apartment. But, as Doctor Robert pointed out, I had trouble connecting with others, and I wanted to step out. I aspired to find another person who could see the world the way I saw it. And there was something about Vinnie's presence that reminded me of my former self. We both struggled to conform to the doctor's advice, yet being together seemed to unleash a newfound freedom. An odd but refreshing feeling of interacting without restraints.

I planned to drive to his apartment complex, only to discover that it was conveniently located just a couple of blocks away from mine. I opted to walk instead, wanting to avoid driving under the influence, whether from alcohol or the aftermath of a hangover. As I approached the complex, I realized that it offered a similar view of the sunset and the sky. I buzzed in, took the elevator to the top floor, and rang Vinnie's doorbell. He welcomed me into his apartment, which was in disrepair. Crumbs littered all over the floor and the walls were smeared with stains.

"Robbie! Are you ready to get drunk? Or are you gonna puke after your first drink?" he said after opening his fridge, which was filled to the brim with bottles of beer.

He grabbed two, and handed one to me. I gazed at the beer in my hand, reluctant to taint myself with a venom like my mom ingested day after day. The contents of the bottles looked more like poison than sustenance. But with Vinnie's hand on my shoulder, I lacked the power to refrain from his offer.

"I think you'll find that I can hold my liquor," I retorted.

"Really? Care to make a bet about that?"

"No, because I know you don't have any money. You probably spend all of it on either beer or bad fashion sense."

And after I said that, I took a swig of my beer, as did Vinnie. But as soon as I was about to swallow, he chugged his beer and threw the bottle straight at me. I narrowly dodged it, but it collided with the wall, shattering on impact. Looking at the wall, I noticed multiple stains from previous bottle impacts. I turned my attention back to Vinnie, who charged towards me, yelling.

"NOW YOU'RE GONNA KEEP YOUR FUCKING MOUTH SHUT WHILE YOU'RE IN MY FUCKING HOME, Y'HEAR?"

Wide-eyed and unsure what to do, I swallowed hard. A sensation churned in my stomach, and I struggled to hold my ground against Vinnie. But I couldn't fight it anymore, and I rushed towards the nearest sink, where I proceeded to vomit.

Vinnie's laughter echoed as I expelled the contents of my stomach. The taste of alcohol lingered, an unpleasant reminder of my lack of tolerance. When Vinnie threw the bottle at me, I might have chugged a large amount of beer in the process, which could have forced anyone to puke, let alone a person unaccustomed to alcohol. I should have known better than to attempt to keep up with Vinnie, who seemed to possess a supernatural ability to handle his liquor.

But Vinnie's laughter turned to tears, and he pulled me into an embrace. I wanted to push him away, but the sincerity in his tears softened my resolve. Though it didn't make me hug him back, because I still felt awful after puking so much. But then he began uttering sentences in between his sobbing.

"I'm so sorry Robbie . . . the truth is . . . I suffer from bipolar disorder. My mood swings can be uncontrollable at times. I've been working on it, taking medication prescribed by a doctor. I didn't mean to hurt you. Please believe me. Don't leave me like everyone else."

His vulnerability touched me, and I found myself saying, "I believe you."

The gratitude in Vinnie's eyes was evident as his tears subsided. However, the aftermath of my excessive puking prevented me from fully reciprocating the hug. Determined to lighten the mood, Vinnie suggested we continue. He went to his fridge and grabbed more beers.

"But maybe we shouldn't be drinking beer," I countered.

"Oh no, you're not getting out of having a good drink. Don't let your puking fool you—once you acquire the taste, it's something you can't resist."

"Then I'll have two beers. I emphasize two. No more after."

"You bet."

And I grabbed a beer. I asked, "Here, do you need help cleaning that up?"

"No, no, don't worry about that. I'll get it, it'll give me some exercise. . . . Here, let's go outside on the veranda, I love watching the sun set."

We walked outside on the balcony and sat down. And at that moment, he began speaking my language. As the sun dipped below the horizon, we delved into conversations that no one else, aside for one, had shown an interest in with me. Movies, video games, books—we explored the realm of art together. I had never encountered someone quite like Vinnie, some-one who shared my imagination and my perspective on the world. The authenticity of our discussion filled the night sky as stars emerged over-head. We gazed at them for what seemed like eternity, losing track of time.

Captivated by the stars, Vinnie spoke poetically, "Death is what allows us to revere the stars. They are beautiful and distant, like sitting on the threshold of eternity, peering into the endless expanse of the night sky. Their distant glow seems to hold the secrets to paradise, illuminating the otherwise pitch-black night. Each star appears as a bright entity, swirling with energy and power, casting its light upon the world below. The stars illuminate our world and impart strength. Do you understand, Robbie?"

"You took the words right out of my mouth."

And at that moment, we felt liberated.

"Hey Robbie, can you get me a beer? I don't think I can get up to grab one."

"Sure, Vinnie."

I went over to the fridge and saw we were out of beer. Apparently I had more than two beers. So I told Vinnie, "Hey, we're out of beers."

"Don't worry, there's more in the closet."

Slightly intoxicated, I made my way to the closet. I opened the door, and sure enough, there were some more cases of beer bottles. But I also noticed something else. It was covered by a tarp. I didn't desire to invade privacy, so I tried to pick up a case. As I fumbled, I inadvertently pulled down the tarp. Vinnie rushed to my side, concerned.

Ignoring his worry, I marveled at the grandeur and imagination before me. The painting contained elements of *Starry Night* by van Gogh, only it was a much different painting. I managed to pick myself up and stand straight, maybe while leaning against a wall.

"Are you a painter, Vinnie? This painting is incredible."

"It's nothing. I consider it a failure. I've been selling some paintings, but it's not selling. I don't know what to do with it. My doctor tells me that painting is a form of escapism, and it can't sustain my means of living and I should avoid it. There are different ways to exercise my life."

"Robert doesn't understand."

"Ahh . . . .I should have known. You were at that complex the same reason I was. But why aren't you listening to the doctor? Don't you want to take his advice?" Vinnie asked.

"This painting embodies everything you spoke about with the stars. The swirls, the brightness, the power—you've transformed those ideas into a visual masterpiece. You have a unique gift."

"Pride is dangerous, Robbie. It can disrupt the status quo, and can stop making things work like clockwork."

His words made me reconsider my own interactions with Robert. Curiosity got the better of me, and I playfully asked, "What's your last name Vinnie? Would it happen to be van Gogh?"

Vinnie chuckled. "No, it's Goldman. My first name was William, but I changed it to Vincent because I love van Gogh's paintings."

"So I'm not the only one who loves *Starry Night*? I can see the inspiration in this, but many aspects are embellished or extracted. You've added your own touch. There's no mountain, there's no town. There's only stars and a glimmer of a sunset. There's no humanity in it, yet there is. It's not a mere imitation; you developed it in a manner that dissociates but shows deference."

"It's sort of like human beings." Vinnie mused.

I pondered his words for a moment before stating, "No, that's just mindless mimicry."

10.

STEP BACK

"Wake up, Robbie."

The light began to glimmer in my eyes, but it seemed brighter than usual. Each attempt to open them was met with a stinging sensation in my eyes, as if lava was being poured on my face. Coupled with this was a massive headache, as though every nudge from Vinnie was a blow from a hammer. I found myself lying on Vinnie's white leather couch.

"Welcome to your first hangover. How does it feel?"

I let out grunts and squeals, too groggy to form coherent words. But I attempted to answer, "Uhhh . . . I . . . ddddoooo . . . gggiiittt . . . mmmmiiii . . ."

"Uh-huh. You were so wasted last night that you passed out on the couch. Listen, I don't mind you staying here and sleeping it off. But I gotta go to work."

I managed to push past my grogginess and vocalize a sentence.

"But . . . today's . . . Saturday."

"That's a work day for me."

Vinnie walked away as he said this. His footsteps faded away to nothing as I heard his apartment door shut. Rather than trying to walk around, I took Vinnie's advice and shut my eyes.

When I awoke, the room was pitch black. I rose to my feet and stumbled towards a light switch, turning it on and realizing it was night outside. I must have slept for about a dozen hours or more. The alcohol had taken a toll on me. The sensitivity to light and the headache had mostly subsided, though I still registered some pain. I made my way to the bathroom and turned the faucet, splashing the icy water in my face. It jolted my senses and revived my awareness.

I noticed multiple empty bottles of pills littered all around the sink. I grabbed one and held it in my hand. The label on the bottle read "Lithium." I took a quick mental note of this, and put it back down. The sight of this troubled me, and I stepped back from the bathroom, walking backwards until my back hit the apartment door. My mind started to wander, but I didn't want it to wander here. I left Vinnie's apartment and returned to my own, lost in my thoughts like a sailor lost at sea.

• • •

I started to see Vinnie more and more as the months passed. He was always an amusing and entertaining person to be around with. I connected with him more than with the people I usually interacted with, including Maddy and Lauro. Strikingly, Vinnie began to get more emaciated over time. When I first met Vinnie he was skinny, but he had a below average build. But now he was so skinny that clothes ballooned on him like bulky snow gear. The process was slow, though I did notice the difference in his body. At first I paid no heed to it, but as time continued to pass, it became increasingly harder to ignore. And I thought it was time to bring it up with him.

I mostly saw Vinnie at his apartment. But I wanted to switch things up, so one day I invited him to my apartment where we could watch my Waterloo Sunset.

He texted me he was here and I opened the door to let him in. He looked like his gaunt self, with his trench coat covering his whole body like armor.

"Robbie! How's college life?"

"About as good as your painting life."

He laughed and started looking around my small apartment.

"You getting in lots of trouble?"

Absolutely not.

"Absolutely!" I decided to change the subject. "How's your job? What do you do exactly?"

"I'm a warehouse worker. The hours are incredibly long. The day you slept at my apartment was actually an eighteen-hour shift. But the idea for the job was actually Doctor Robert's. He explained to me the reason why I get these intense mood swings was that I have too much time on my hands. When I have more time for myself, my brain resorts to anger or anguish as it can't handle loneliness. When I have something to do, it takes a weight off my mind so I don't have to think."

"I see. Is there something wrong with thinking? Is there something wrong with being alone?"

Vinnie scoffed and stared at me. "Human beings aren't meant to be alone, Robbie. We're meant to be together and fit in with each other."

I narrowed my eyes. "Is that why you admire van Gogh? Because his artwork fits in with everything else?"

He grimaced and opened his mouth. I thought he would launch into one of his fits, but he stopped himself. "I sense a little hostility here. But don't worry, I brought beer, and that always makes everything better."

I noticed he was holding a case of beer. It made me ponder the night I got intoxicated with him. I asked myself why I drank the alcohol he offered me, and I realized that there wasn't a reason to drink it, and I just drank it to imitate him. I scarcely remembered the moment, but it was almost euphoric and exhilarating. The alcohol blinded my ability to think clearly, and I lost control, like being trapped in a dark cave, unable to see. But the loss of control was unique, a feeling that was unknown to me. Maybe that was why so many people craved it, because it fractured the control necessary to conform to others. But the act of drinking also ironically became an act of conformity, a certain expectation of surviving in a clockwork society.

We both settled into chairs on the balcony, and he handed me a beer bottle. I slowly took it and opened it. I was about to take a swig, but I found the strength to put it down on the ground. I valued my ability to reason more than my need to conform. And I doubt Vinnie noticed, as he was too busy guzzling down his own beer. I wanted to ask about the overabundance of pill bottles in his apartment, or his atrophied state, but I lacked the strength to do so.

But Vinnie did eventually stop drinking and said to me, "Okay, it's your turn now. Tell me what you see when you look at this sunset."

I looked at the dark red sunset, engulfing the cityscape with its potent hue.

"I see what I desire to be."

Confused, Vinnie asked, "What do you mean?"

"I behold my aspirations within this sunset's embrace, a tapestry of resplendent power that blankets the landscape in a crimson glow. The world pauses in reverent admiration, drawn to its commanding presence, yearning to embody its essence. Do you understand what I'm saying?"

"Yes, it's as if we reside in paradise." And Vinnie continued to drink.

"Why do you drink, Vinnie?"

"I don't know. I never really thought about it. But maybe because it feels good. It's a way of dealing with my problems."

"Won't it provide you with more problems? Won't it potentially cause kidney disease, liver disease, and most importantly, limit your ability to make decisions?"

"Ehhh . . . maybe . . . but I'm here for a good time, not a long time. . . ."

I laughed and wondered how much longer Vinnie could last drinking so much alcohol all the time.

I then asked, "If you drink alcohol to deal with your problems, why don't you just deal with your problems, instead of resorting to alcohol?"

"The same reason . . . the same reason you stare at this sunset all the time. There are some problems that you can't solve."

I thought about this, and wondered if Vinnie was right, and if I did over-rely on this sunset. Was it wrong to possess an outlet? It was hardly more harmful than Vinnie's excessive drinking. But were there more productive things I could have been doing instead of this? Yet if I did something like playing video games, reading, or watching movies, was that much different? Would my life improve if I simply used all my time with other people instead? But then wouldn't I just crave more time for myself? What was the answer? I couldn't think of one.

As my mind continued to wander, Vinnie continued to guzzle beer and soon fell asleep in his chair. I carried him inside and laid him on the couch. In the morning, Vinnie awoke groaning and yelling in pain. I hurried over, but then he told me to "chill" and explained he was suffering from a hangover. He eventually arose, and thanked me for letting him stay the night. I told him that it was the same thing he did for me. The same thing friends should do to each other.

• • •

I sat in a booth at Joe Schmoe's once again. I decided to introduce Maddy and Lauro to Vinnie, and I thought this would be as good a place as any. The bar was its usual crowded self, with its dim lighting and terrible music. All four of us agreed to meet at the bar at 9:00 p.m. But I told Vinnie to show up at 8:30 because there was something I wanted to discuss with him. I finally worked up the strength to bring it up with him. But it wasn't something, rather someone: Doctor Robert.

It divided me that someone with so much wisdom could rub me the wrong way. Whenever he talked, I couldn't help but listen and believe what he said. But whenever I thought about what he said, I bit my tongue. I kept flip-flopping back and forth from trusting to not trusting him. It was like I was both capable and incapable of change.

As I mulled over my thoughts, Vinnie walked over to my booth, but he stumbled and actually hit his knee into another booth. After a brief remark about the pain, he sat down across from me. It had only been a couple of weeks since he slept at my apartment, but he looked even thinner, paler, and noticeably more haggard. The life was sucked out of him. I had grasped just enough power to begin our discussion, but he started before me.

"Hey buddy! What's going on?"

"Nothing much. Did you recover from that hangover fast?"

"Oh, absolutely. I'm a master at this point. They always hurt like a bitch, but I get over it fast . . . Doctor Robert says . . ."

"It seems you can't do anything without mentioning Doctor Robert's advice," I interrupted.

"What?"

"Well, that's what I wanted to talk to you about. What are your thoughts on Doctor Robert?"

"What about him? He's a doctor. More specifically, he's our doctor."

I lowered my head, staring down at the table for several seconds. Then I finally put my head back up to ask, "Have you noticed anything off about him? Any sign that makes you question his ability as a doctor?"

Confused, Vinnie narrowed his eyebrows and asked, "No, why?" He smirked and explained, "Robbie, don't be like that. There is a stigma about mental health professionals. You shouldn't add to it. Doctors are designed to help, not hinder."

"What stigma are you referring to? Is it the fact that pharmaceutical drugs are a trillion-dollar industry? Or is it the fact that psychology degrees are some of the most popular majors for undergraduates?"

"This is about the medicine, isn't it? Have you been taking your meds?"

I sighed. "He prescribed me some. I haven't taken any."

"Why?"

"Well, to give an example, I took a look at your pill bottles, and I noticed you've been taking lithium. Lithium is a potent drug. It can cause dehydration and it affects your metabolism, which might explain your gaunt appearance. You have a lot of empty pill bottles. Are you taking them as prescribed?"

Vinnie placed his hands on the table. He squeezed them into fists. He grimaced severely.

"Doctor Robert said to increase my dosage due to how severe my outbursts are."

"You didn't answer my question."

He slammed his fists against the table, and he stood to yell, "OF COURSE I'M TAKING MORE THAN PRESCRIBED!"

The whole bar was silent, with every patron staring at us. Vinnie looked around, then looked down, and sat back down. After a few more seconds, the bar was back to its rambunctious self.

"That's concerning, Vinnie. If you take too much, you can get lithium toxicity or you can even overdose. . . . Didn't you research any of this?"

"Of course I did. The diagnosis made sense to me. And I'm only taking more because I need it. Because it makes me feel good . . . Robbie, Robert is a doctor. He's had extensive medical education. I'm sure he knows what he's doing."

"So as long as he's a doctor, that makes him correct? It's not about the science, it's about the scientist?"

Just then, Maddy and Lauro walked over to our booth and sat next to Vinnie. Vinnie and I dropped our discussion. What surprised me was how fast Vinnie connected with them. He was smiling and laughing along with Maddy and Lauro. Knowing Vinnie and the nights we shared, I believed he wasn't really interested in superficial conversation. But there he was, pulling it off like a magician doing a trick. It made me wonder if he was even happy at that moment.

I caught a snippet of conversation. "The pills Robert prescribed me make me feel so much better," Lauro stated.

Maddy and Vinnie were about to jump in, but I jumped in first. "Does Doctor Robert get paid to prescribe medications to you?"

Lauro sat for a moment and then replied, "I don't know. I didn't really think about it. . . . Why, Robbie?"

I was about to point out the obvious parallel between the amount of money Doctor Robert would receive and the amount of medications Lauro received. But my power to jump back in waned, and I simply replied, "Nothing. Never mind."

At this point, a waitress walked over and asked us if we wanted any drinks. I replied in the negative when she asked me.

Vinnie responded, "What this man means is that he absolutely wants a drink. Give him a shot of vodka."

The waitress left. Vinnie launched into laughter and said, "You should have seen this guy a few months ago. He was drinking beers left and right."

Maddy and Lauro laughed along with Vinnie. Maddy explained, "I'm glad you've stepped out of your shell, Robbie. It took you years, but you've finally found how to be like everyone else."

Just then the waitress put a shot of vodka on the table. I looked into the clear liquid and remembered my mom drinking it. I remembered all the anguish that caused her to drink it. And I remembered all the anguish that drinking it caused her. I saw all of the world's problems reside in that drink.

And then I looked up. I saw Vinnie, Lauro, and Maddy eagerly waiting for me to drink the shot. I lacked the power to step back. So I grabbed the shot glass, and drank the liquid that burned my body and soul.

THE REPUBLIC

I settled into the worn leather chair in Doctor Robert's office, my body tense with anticipation. The soft glow of the dimmed lights cast shadows across the room, creating an ambience of introspection.

"So Robbie, what did you do for the weekend?"

"I visited the Guardian's Hideaway with some friends. It's a green but well-trodden trail that connects from a nearby mountain. It's a popular location because it's not too far away from the city. The trail led us to a large, deep cave at the end. While my friends were captivated by the cave, I was more intrigued by the surrounding flora. Eventually, I decided to explore the cave. My steps echoed against the brisk stone walls. The air carried a damp scent, mingling with the faint sound of dripping water. I found my friends admiring its walls. They refused to leave, claiming an attachment to the place. One even jokingly suggested I return to 'my cave' and leave them behind. Remembering your advice, I stayed in the cave, experiencing what felt like eternity. When we finally left, my eyes struggled to adjust to the outside light, nearly causing me to fall down a hill. It made me realize that I don't wish to embark on any more cave expeditions. Social gatherings, in the end, feel like being trapped in another form of a cave."

Doctor Robert inquired, "I take it you did not have fun?"

My mind wandered. My thoughts drifted to questions that plagued me. The weight of my skepticism settled heavily on my shoulders, making it difficult to express. But I had to try. The words struggled to escape my lips as I grappled with my conflicted thoughts.

"No." I replied. "It wasn't just an eyesight issue. Most of the hike was filled with friends indulging in mindless gossip, labeling individuals as mentally ill or strange. I struggle to comprehend how people can talk all day without saying anything."

"Human beings are social creatures, Robbie. We crave social interactions and build communities based on shared rules and boundaries. Conformity allows us to form communities and foster happiness. When people transgress these boundaries, people have a tendency to discuss their stifled happiness. You must learn to respect other people's experiences, Robbie. Remember, man is the measure of all things."

"There's an old adage: great minds discuss ideas, small minds discuss people," I retorted.

"So do you consider yourself a great mind?"

"Well, you see, Doctor, I brought a book this time. Perhaps you've heard of it. It's Plato's *Republic*. There's an allegory in there that I'm sure you're familiar with."

"I am. So, to you, your friends led you out of one cave, and to another."

I explained, "No, I've escaped the cave. Most people are too ignorant to isolate and educate themselves. They prefer to flock together in crowds, clinging to vices that offer fleeting happiness. You might argue that I live in a cave, but true intelligence is a solitary pursuit. It relies on individual abilities, not collective association or imitation. As Plato suggests, most dwell in a cave, while only a few can escape. I only need to point to you and therapy. I haven't been taking the prescribed medication, because I don't trust you. Every time I see Vinnie, he appears different, as if his very soul is leaving his body. He frequently erupts in anger, his complexion pale, his demeanor frail. You are making Vinnie's life worse. Yet they all embrace you wholeheartedly, as if stuck in a cave."

Doctor Robert responded, "Well, Robbie, I also planned to discuss *The Republic* as well. I have my own copy right here, the same edition as yours. Please turn to Book Three. It states that a doctor may only treat sickness if they have experienced it themselves. And I have been sick, Robbie. At a young age, I faced extraordinary hardships. I lost my father, never experiencing a father's love, or the comfort it brings to help a poor boy sleep at night. This took its toll, leaving me feeling like an outsider among my peers. I was bullied. I was lost. But I chose medicine to help others, to be the support I never had growing up. I can assure you, my entire existence is dedicated to healing you and ensuring your well-being.

"Robbie, you missed the crucial point that Plato's *Republic* conveys. Every aspect of the Kallipolis, from the producers to the guardians to the philosopher-kings, exists to serve others. *The Republic* is centered around justice, which entails fulfilling your role for the betterment of society. You think that intelligence is a solitary act, but that's not Plato's point. Plato advocates for dialectics, conversations that flourish through interactions with others. You live in a society, Robbie. Without others, you will lose yourself, humility, and the power in your life. Others can provide strength, but only if you navigate the boundaries set by society."

My brows furrowed as I mulled over his words. These ideas, so deeply rooted in Plato's philosophy, had rattled my worldview. The weight of the conversation settled upon me, stirring a mixture of curiosity and doubt within my heart.

"No, no, no . . . ."

"Robbie, you're about to cry. Here, please take some tissues."

"Okay."

"I know this is difficult for you. But remember, you're not alone in this journey. Everyone experiences this conversion process at some point in their lives. Therapy exists to help us recognize our fallibilities and overcome them; it's a humbling experience. And remember, this isn't a one-sided endeavor. Plato's *Republic* speaks of escaping the cave, but we must also consider the stories of Socrates' other students, Alcibiades and Critias. They believed they had escaped the cave, only to become rulers turned tyrants, imposing harsh and anti-democratic rules. And many like them followed: Hitler, Stalin, Mao. The most evil and vicious acts done across the centuries were due to people who thought they 'escaped the cave.' Imagine how many lives could have been saved if they had access to mental health treatments, allowing them to work past issues rather than perpetrating atrocities. Imagine how many artists could have been saved from suffering from their demons alone. They could have found help."

With a mix of anger and sadness etched on my face, I shouted, "No, there's nothing wrong with me. I'M NOT A FREAK!"

Once again, Doctor Robert replied in a serene and steady manner. "You're not a freak. There's nothing inherently wrong with you. When I look at you, I see a reflection of myself. However, you possess certain differences that set you apart from the rest of the population. One must understand their differences to journey through life more smoothly. Then they can fit in, find friends, and find love. It's something anyone would want, but it requires effort and self-reflection. And that's where I come in. I help you reach your full potential, so everyone can see what I see in you. Remember, one must do what is good for the republic."

I fell silent, absorbing his words.

"I'm sorry . . . I never could have imagined that . . . someone like you . . . would be helping me. Now I realize that perhaps . . . I'm not alone. That perhaps to fit in . . . to imitate . . . isn't something to dismiss. I see you beat me at my own game. You proposed a reading of *The Republic* I hadn't considered. . . . You've proposed to me an argument that I cannot refute. The anti-thesis . . . has overcome the thesis."

"Then do I have your trust?"

"Yes."

No.

AT ETERNITY'S GATE

"His sadness will last forever," I remarked.

"I wonder if he's been going to therapy," Lauro pondered.

"I mean, I don't really feel like helping him. . . . Someone qualified should help him," Maddy added.

"He probably has ADHD . . ."

"Or bipolar . . ."

"Maybe mania . . ."

"No! Epilepsy! He definitely has epilepsy!"

"What's epilepsy?" I inquired, turning to Maddy.

"A neurological disorder that causes seizures."

"But Vinnie doesn't have seizures." I pointed out.

"He has intense mood swings. They're the same thing!"

"No, a seizure is entirely different from acting angrily."

"Well, that doesn't matter. I just feel uncomfortable when he's around, and how I feel is what matters. . . . .Besides, whatever his condition is, it's probably worse because he drinks and smokes so much," asserted Maddy.

"Definitely," agreed Lauro, taking another swig of beer. We sat in a booth near the back of Joe Schmoe's, where conversations around Vinnie's condition filled the air. Trusting Doctor Robert more had brought me closer to my friends, and I saw them frequently. They always used the excuse of being busy to avoid me. But thanks to Doctor Robert, I learned that it was just an indirect way of saying they didn't like my company and were too afraid to be honest. I found myself using the word "like" more often. Doctor Robert advised me to identify my feelings and follow them, unless I felt like being honest. He explained that most people don't communicate honestly, so I should adhere to social cues and norms to build relationships. In truth, I didn't comprehend what I was doing that brought me closer to Maddy and Lauro, but I just acted how they acted and deeper connections formed. It was confusing much of the time, but I respected my doctor's expertise. He had obviously relied on more than just his feelings to diagnose my disorder.

After spending about two hours discussing Vinnie's condition, we couldn't decide what disorder he possessed. With nothing else to talk about, we decided to leave the bar. Lauro and Maddy planned to discuss the matter with their other friends, so they left together while I walked back home.

Entering my apartment, I flicked on the lights, but the brightness hurt my eyes. Spending the evening in the dimly lit bar had likely affected my eyesight. I went into the closet, like I did so many times before, and grabbed the revolver. Opting to keep the lights off, I settled in a chair on the veranda. I had missed my Waterloo Sunset because I was with my friends, and I didn't feel its power or light tonight. Sitting in the darkness for an unknown duration, I realized I wasn't happy.

Despite gaining friends, improving my relationships with Lauro and Maddy, and becoming a normal and productive member of society, a sick and strange darkness seeped into my soul every night. I had been Doctor Robert's patient for six months now, and though I said I was better, I was not actually better. Thoughts of suicide frequented my mind, but I had to maintain a smile and put on a happy face, just like any other "normal" person would. I realized that no one can be completely happy in this world, regardless of the power one wields.

During moments like this, I yearned for a mother or father to confide in, someone who wouldn't claim to be busy. So I resorted to the next best thing—I turned to my mother's journal in search of answers. Surprisingly, I had missed a passage before that resonated within me like a perfectly harmonized piano key.

Robbie has just finished fifth grade. I'm so proud of him. His reading comprehension has improved significantly, and he's begun reading on his own without my prompting. He's taken a keen interest in books and discusses them with me constantly. Other kids his age are getting into trouble, but not my Robbie. I wish I could see him come of age, but I don't think I have much longer now. Nevertheless, I'm proud of Robbie. I know he has the strength to do what is right.

Upon reading those words, I realized I had forgotten to take my medication. Walking to the bathroom, I switched on the light, opened the medicine cabinet, and retrieved the bottle. I opened the bottle and rolled a pill into my hand, ready to swallow. But then I asked myself why I was taking the pill. "To fix a mental disorder." But how could Doctor Robert diagnose a biological problem without examining my biology? With this in mind, I threw the pills into the toilet, flushing them away. I knew I would face withdrawal symptoms, but it was preferable to subjecting myself to the uncertain fate the pills held.

As I left the bathroom, my phone began to ring. Maddy was calling me. I answered, and she struggled to deliver some heartbreaking news—Vinnie had passed away. He had overdosed on his medication.

• • •

"If he just took therapy more seriously . . ."

"If he just kept taking his meds . . ."

Then Lauro and Maddy said, almost unanimously, "Maybe he wouldn't be dead."

"Didn't he overdose? How would that have helped?" I asked. And Maddy and Lauro both shushed me.

We were at Vinnie's funeral, and these were all the words anyone could say. I was in that same church where I mourned my mom so many years ago. The pews were so filled to the brim that some had to stand in the back. The building's walls were as boisterous as the bar's. A kaleidoscope of colors still flooded the room from the stained glass windows. And that giant man on the cross was still overlooking us all. Maddy and Lauro were sitting next to me, and I mainly chatted with them, but the conversations I overheard in the neighboring pews were the same as the ones I heard from Lauro and Maddy. "If he ever needed anything, he could have asked," one would say, or "It's so sad because so many people cared about him," another would say. And I couldn't stop thinking about the fact that when I met Vinnie, he was stuck in his apartment all day, and it didn't seem like anyone was interested in actually caring about him.

The funeral was long and dull, mainly due to so many "friends and family" appearing on the podium proclaiming how well they knew Vinnie and how much they were going to miss him. Many of these people I never heard of, as Vinnie never spoke of them. And as the acquaintances of Vinnie kept cycling through their stories on the podium, it looked as though they put more effort into convincing people they cared about Vinnie, rather than actually caring about Vinnie. But all of this was lost on the people around me in the pews, as they were seemingly enraptured by all the proclaiming.

After the festivity was over, Maddy and Lauro wanted to stay and chat with Vinnie's supposed friends and family. But they weren't actually Vinnie's friends and family, and as such, I lacked the power to waste time with masqueraders who put more attention into imitation rather than true connection.

I left the church and I quickly walked to my car. As I opened the car door, I felt a tap on the shoulder. It was Maddy.

"Where you going?"

"Home."

"Maybe you wanna go see Doctor Robert?"

"No, I don't feel like . . . I'm not going to see him."

"Have you been taking your meds?"

After Maddy said that, I glared at her, jumped into my car, and closed the door. She stood for a second, and then walked back into the church. It momentarily made me feel bad, but I had the power to drive away.

• • •

Days after Vinnie's funeral, things still ran like clockwork. I was with Maddy and Lauro at the same bar in the back, and they engaged in the same asinine conversations as before.

"He probably has autism . . ."

"Yeah, I feel so uncomfortable around him. . . . Even though I know nothing about his biology, I'm pretty sure he has a biological disorder. . . ."

This conversation got me thinking about why and how I was diagnosed. Psychology is the study of human behavior, and it lists autism as a biological disorder. People say that autistic brains are fundamentally different than the brains of others. However, Doctor Robert didn't perform any type of biological test on me. He didn't examine my brain. He made an extrapolation based on my experiences, which isn't science. It was subjective and contextual, making it impossible to label it as a biological disorder. Science is supposed to be objective and quantifiable, but Doctor Robert didn't perform any objective test on me. How could he say that my brain was different without examining it? I did research on my own, and learned that there is no test to diagnose someone with a mental illness. How could someone claim that someone's behavior is wrong on a subjective basis? How could someone diagnose a person with a biological disorder without any biological evidence? Some psychologists even admit that it is subjective, and if that's the case, then how is it a science? If you argue on a subjective basis, then why can't you dismiss it on a subjective basis? I started to come to terms with the fact that the problem wasn't with me, but with how people interacted with each other.

I then started to ponder some of the ideas that Doctor Robert told me. Like when he said, "*However, what I can promise you is this: see that degree hanging on the wall? It took me eight years of rigorous education to earn that degree. . . . I'm reading this book, right now, to better myself as a doctor, to see the other side. I desire to understand any distrust you have. I want to be the doctor who made you change your mind about doctors.*"

This might have sounded nice rhetorically, but it lacked a solid rational foundation. If you broke down what he was saying, removing all the rhetoric, he said that he spent a great deal of effort studying his field and wanted to understand any distrust I might have. But that meant nothing. The amount of effort put into something does not dictate knowledge. True knowledge is expressed through action. He said he "desired" to understand, but why should that be trusted? Why should I take him at his word? Why should I trust Doctor Robert simply because he is a doctor?

And then when I asked him about his office space, and his submissive secretary's clothing, he said, "*The architecture and design that clients desire for their homes can be just as unconventional as my office space. It is simply an expression of personal taste and comfort. As for my secretary, it is not my place to dictate her choice of clothing.*"

Again, he said nothing of substance. He didn't address my concerns, and deflected them instead. He said that his office was "an expression of personal taste and comfort." But that meant nothing. Why did he choose to paint his office black and white? He didn't explain it. And he didn't explain why his secretary dressed in such an erotic way. Could that really be dismissed solely by personal expression? A haunting thought occurred to me. Could Doctor Robert have done something to her to make her that way?

Then other words that he spoke to me began to surface. "*As a student of neuroscience, I understand the intricacies of the human brain. . . . And if people leave your life repeatedly, or if people don't want to be around you, it's a sign that something might be wrong with your brain.*"

These words were laced with poor rhetorical techniques, rather than substantive ones. He argued from his authority and didn't have any evidence to back it up. Just because he was a doctor, just because he studied neuroscience, didn't make him automatically right. If the brain has a normal function, then what is the normal function? Isn't every human and how they interact different?

And then when we discussed Plato's *Republic,* he explained, "*You think that intelligence is a solitary act, but that's not Plato's point. Plato advocates for dialectics, conversations that flourish through interactions with others. You live in a society, Robbie. Without others, you will lose yourself, humility, and the power in your life. Others can provide strength, but only if you navigate the boundaries set by society.*"

Doctor Robert performed a rhetorical sleight of hand. He argued that engaging with other people is an act of intelligence. I needed to respect other people's "boundaries" and that would give me strength. He argued from points of Plato's philosophy, equating Plato's endorsement on dialogues to an endorsement of conformity. Why would a desire to engage with other people's ideas equate to following societal rules and norms? Socrates, Plato's teacher, was executed for not following societal rules and norms. Plato once said, "Those who are able to see beyond the shadows and lies of their culture will never be understood, let alone believed, by the masses." This isn't rooted in Plato's philosophy, nor is Robert's argument sound. He didn't explain how society or others can give you strength. He didn't explain what boundaries are or how it creates a stable society. He was purposely vague in order for me to believe what he said. He was more of a politician, who utilizes language to make you believe him rather than to engage with the ideas presented.

As I reflected on all this, I realized that the whole field of psychology was a lie. It was built on rhetoric and faulty logic, rather than substance. It was built on pseudoscience, rather than science. It was built on subjective judgments, rather than facts and evidence. Doctor Robert acted no different than a sophist from Plato's *Republic.* He proposed that justice is the advantage of the stronger. He proposed that justice, and what is right, is defined by what is popular.

And the more I thought about this, the more I thought about why it seemed Vinnie had killed himself. Vinnie always defended Doctor Robert, always did what he told him to do, and yet he still killed himself. He overdosed from his medications. He had piles of pill bottles at his house. And no one thought that would hurt him? Vinnie began to get more and more gaunt as the months went by. Therapy is meant to improve a person, not worsen them. And if that's the case, why did Vinnie not get better, but worse? The whole reason he went to Doctor Robert was because he had intense mood swings. But those didn't stop after seeing Robert; it was always a constant. Doctor Robert was supposed to help Vinnie through his problems, but Vinnie's problems only worsened, and he was still happy to see the doctor.

Just then, my lapse in thought was interrupted by a comment from Lauro.

"Hey Maddy, what's that mark you have on your neck there?"

Lauro pointed to a blemish on the left side of Maddy's neck. Her eyes looked around the bar, seemingly seeking answers in her surroundings.

But she finally said, "Oh don't you remember, Lauro? You gave that to me when you were kissing me."

"But how come I don't remember it?" Lauro retorted, with an edge in his voice.

Maddy momentarily avoided eye contact, but then responded, "You probably were drunk and forgot everything the next morning."

Lauro clenched his fists, but before Lauro could reply, Maddy said, "Have you been taking your meds, Lauro? Please don't take your anger out on me. You need to get your problems together."

Just then Lauro began to cry, and Maddy hugged him.

"I haven't been taking any. Doctor Robert told me not to take any more," Lauro stated.

"Why did he tell you to stop?" I blurted out. Maddy and Lauro both stared at me with wide eyes.

"Well . . . he probably doesn't want me to be dependent on the drugs."

I replied, "Well, I guess you're dependent on them now then, huh?"

"No. I also got to him to explain the problems I've been feeling."

"So then I guess you're dependent on him then, huh?"

"Robbie, Robert's a doctor. He's there to help me. I am not under his thumb."

Lauro quickly rose from his seat and dashed away from our table, most likely walking to the bathroom. Maddy sighed and closed her eyes.

"Great job, by the way," I joked.

Maddy opened her eyes and scowled at me.

"The way you deflected his question, and focused more on his issues. Is that the ideal relationship Doctor Robert has brought you? Where we are unable to communicate with each other? Where we have to focus more on how we feel rather than how it is?"

"You know, Robbie, ever since we became friends, all you've ever done is make jokes at our expense. You tried to be different, but now you're going back to old habits. In a session I had with Doctor Robert, we wondered what the point was of us being friends."

I lowered my eyebrows. "You didn't answer my question. What are you hiding from Lauro? You can't fool me, Maddy."

She was silent for a while and looked at the table, searching for the right words.

But then a harrowing thought eclipsed my mind. I was reminded of Ashley Lawson, Doctor Robert's salacious secretary. And then I finally formed a thought and spoke it out loud. "No, it can't be. Don't tell me Doctor Robert did that to you?"

She then looked up, refusing to speak.

"Why, Maddy? Why?"

"I didn't do anything with Doctor Robert."

"What about Lauro?"

"There's nothing to tell. I told you, I didn't do anything with Robert."

"What if I tell him that I think you did?"

"No, you can't!"

"I have to. I can't just dismiss this."

Maddy bit her lip and then quickly stated, "He won't believe you. And if you do tell him, I'll . . . I'll just tell him that you tried to come on to me just now."

Stunned, I couldn't verbalize a sentence. Maddy thought her life was falling apart, and she was trying to save it any way she could. Maddy had been my friend for years, but she seemed willing to throw that all away just to defend Doctor Robert. And after a minute, I finally uttered, "I can't believe what I'm hearing. How could you let him do this to you?"

"Robbie . . . he's a doctor . . . When are you going to accept that doctors are supposed to help you, not harm you?"

Then I was silent. I thought about everything I knew about Doctor Robert since I met him. The way his office overwhelmed you in white, seemingly forcing you to think internally. The way his secretary was so submissive towards me, and probably Robert. The way that Robert was able to know everything about me, and what I was going to discuss beforehand. The way that Robert was able to guilefully reject my objections, and turn the objections towards me. The way that he acted more as a rhetorician, not addressing anything I said. The way that Vinnie got worse rather than better after seeing him. The way that he was probably taking advantage of Lauro and other patients. The way that he probably sexually abused Maddy. After thinking on all these ideas, I was convinced. Robert was not who he said he was. I'd always had doubts about him, and I lacked the power to do anything about it then. But I had the power to do something now.

In the midst of our conversation, I abruptly stood up and walked out of the bar. Maddy started to flag me down, begging me to stay. But my mind was made up and I left her there, not looking back. I looked back so many times before, but today I wasn't going to.

The only thing on my mind was one person: Doctor Robert. The more I thought about it, the more I thought about all the things he could have done. But I realized this might have been a leap in logic, and I needed more information before I did anything rash. I had a plan that could give me that information. It was risky, but I possessed power and purpose that I never had before.

• • •

I stared at my Waterloo Sunset. Normally I was powerless in my gaze, but today I possessed the power to do something. It was a quiet moment before a raging storm. I sat on my veranda, dressed to leave immediately, as I was about to enact my plan to learn more about our good doctor. I tried researching the doctor online, but I found nothing suspicious. I tried researching my state's repository of criminal records, but I found nothing there either. All I could find online were positive reviews, communicating glowing praise for Doctor Robert. As such, I had to do something myself if I was going to confirm my suspicions. My plan was risky, as I was about to break the law, so I thought I'd take in a sunset to prepare me for what was to come.

I sat at Eternity's Gate. But I didn't feel fear. I didn't feel sadness. I didn't feel anything. I had an obligation to do what was right. It was beyond any feeling that I had. My feelings had corrupted who I was, but I wasn't going to let my feelings rule over me. Today I had a purpose, and I was intent on following through on a purpose that was above me. Things were no longer running like clockwork, and that gave me a newfound power.

I took a deep breath. I grasped my phone firmly, anticipation flowing through my veins. With determined swipes, I accessed my contacts and scrolled to Doctor Robert. He had willingly provided his contact information, extending a line of communication between us in case I needed it. Little did he know, I was about to sever that connection.

Pressing the call button, I raised the phone to my ear, listening intently as it emitted a ringing sound. Each ring seemed to amplify the weight of my decision, urging me to retreat. But I pushed through, refusing to let my feelings overpower me.

"Hello, Robbie, what can I do for you?"

As his voice flowed through the line, a shiver ran down my spine. I didn't know what to say. I paused for so long until he said, "Robbie?"

"Robbie . . . I mean Robert, I'm not feeling too well . . . I mean, there's something I need to tell you."

"Why? What's wrong?"

I continued, "Therapy isn't right for me. Maybe I should have called the secretary to cancel my appointments, but I thought you should hear it from me. I just thought I'd tell you that I won't be seeing you anymore."

"I'm sorry to hear that. Can you explain why you feel this way?"

"It's because of Vinnie, Robert. He was a loyal patient of yours, always supporting you and your methods. But he still felt powerless and seemed to end his life. And for that reason, your methods will not help me foster growth as a person."

"Robbie, I understand how you feel, but therapy can still be enlightening for you. Just because Vinnie ended his life, doesn't mean you will . . ."

I predicted that he would react this way. His words were always laced with familiar rhetorical and manipulative techniques. He was acting as a salesman at the moment, combating my objections. His counterargument might have been right, of course, but now was not the time or place for a sales speech. Now was the time for a different approach. I interrupted him.

"Look, I'm sure you have much to say. But words won't cut it anymore. Thank you, and have a good night."

"Wait! Listen, why don't we talk about this in one of your sessions, and we can have a face-to-face discussion about this? Now's not the time or place to discuss this."

"Look, like I said, I'm not interested anymore. And I might consider discussing this with Lauro and Maddy to stop seeing you as well."

"Okay, why don't you come over to my place right now? I can see you're upset, and I want to ease your concerns."

Finally, the question I wanted him to ask.

"I don't know, Robert, this seems a little informal. You sure it's okay to see you like this?"

"Nonsense. Caring about my patients is a priority of mine. Vinnie's death, I'm sure, was a shock, and I want to help you. It might be unorthodox, but I'd love to meet right now to help process your feelings. Therapy is right for you, and I want to prove that to you."

"Well, as long as you're okay with it, then I am."

"Perfect. You can find me at this address . . ."

But I was more than okay with it. He fell into my little snare, and now I knew where he lived.

• • •

I drove over to Doctor Robert's house, which was more like a mansion. That might have been an exaggeration, but it certainly was extravagant, vast, and grand. It was two stories high, and it exuded a lack of color. The roof was all black, but each side of the house was all white. It possessed the same milky color that his office did. It lacked any heart or vigor, and looked empty inside. But even so, I drove to the front entrance, and sauntered over to the front door, gazing at Doctor Robert's dwelling.

The door, locked with a keypad, presented a challenge. I knew I had to see him input the code if my plan was to succeed. I laid three careful knocks at the front door, waiting for an answer. He finally opened the door and greeted me exuberantly. He wore his usual black dress shirt and black dress pants.

He said warmly with a smile, "Hello, Robbie." But if my suspicions were correct, that smile was more sinister than it looked.

His greeting gave me pause. I looked down.

"Look, Robert, maybe this was a bad idea. I shouldn't have come here."

I turned around, started walking away, and he took the bait and walked in front of me, with the door closing behind him. He put his hand on my shoulder.

"No. As I said before, I am here to get you back to running like clockwork. I'm sure Vinnie's death took a lot out of you, and I'm here to help."

We walked back to the door together, and I saw him input the code 1978. I said that over and over in my head until I memorized it. The door opened, and I once again entered a brave new world.

The interior of his house manifested another expanse of stark whiteness, every surface devoid of any other color, yet alive with the vibrancy of art. The walls were adorned with an eclectic array of paintings, album covers, and various artworks, each piece telling its own story amid the sea of white. On my left, a vast library beckoned to me, its shelves brimming with books that whispered the secrets of the world. On my right, a collection of CDs glittered like jewels, each case a portal to a different melody, inviting me to explore the rhythm of his soul. If I were to own a house, I'd probably mimic the same decorations that Doctor Robert furnished, as it imitated the same non-mimicked imitations that I mimicked, even if I shouldn't mimic for the sake of it.

"You still listen to CDs," I remarked.

"It's the only way to listen to music," he quipped.

"It doesn't seem to be the normal way," I muttered under my breath.

He led me to his living room, where a shiny leather couch, and a gigantic big-screen TV resided. We both rested on the couch.

I couldn't silence my next quip. "You seem to be living in the lap of luxury."

"These material possessions don't nearly grant me as much satisfaction as when I'm giving satisfaction to a patient."

I'm sure it's at the forefront of his mind when he's cashing his checks.

"But enough about me. We're here to talk about you. You mentioned that you're uncertain about the value of therapy for you. I must admit, I'm somewhat surprised. You've made remarkable progress, so why would you want to stop now?"

"Before I answer, let me ask you something: has any patient of yours stopped using you as their doctor?"

"No, never. They might initially stop, but they always come back. We all grow and change, and therapy facilitates that growth. As such, all my patients all have reasons to come back. My patients continue to rely on me because they cannot navigate their lives alone. They need guidance."

He uttered that last sentence with a hint of ridicule, the same sort of ridicule that I'd thrown towards others. It gave me greater confidence and power to do what I was about to do next.

"Well then, allow me to be your first patient who leaves you. I have the power to grow and lead my life without you. I appreciate the time and energy you've invested in me, but I no longer need you. Vinnie's death confirmed that therapy doesn't always yield positive outcomes."

"Robbie, are you off your meds?"

"As a matter of fact, I am. My mind doesn't need altering from mind-altering drugs."

"Those mind-altering drugs are there to correct chemical imbalances in your brain, Robbie. So you can behave like everyone else."

"But I don't want to be like everyone else."

Robert paused, and when he was about to speak, I interrupted him.

"I've done some research on my own doctor. Chemical imbalance theory has been widely discredited by scientists as lacking evidence and sufficient reason to support it. The measurements of chemicals in the brain are difficult to quantify. For example, every individual can function with their own amount of serotonin. There is no established threshold of how much serotonin or other chemicals in the brain are needed. So if there is no established threshold, then why would you prescribe medications to alter the amount of chemicals in the brain? Even if you could answer that question, chemicals in the brain don't cause anguish. Situational factors, like the death of a loved one, can cause distress. And if that can cause a disorder, then that would mean the root cause of a mental disorder is not a chemical imbalance. What makes a person depressed or not depressed doesn't boil down to the amount of chemicals in the brain. Yet pharmaceutical companies make billions in profit from the masses who take these prescriptions. Look what happened to Vinnie; his mind was altered to a point that he was no longer a human being. He erupted into bouts of anger constantly. He couldn't live with that fact, so he ended his pain, permanently."

Robert paused, clearly caught off-guard, but oddly also with a touch of a smile.

"What Vinnie did was regrettable, but he represents an outlier in what psychiatry aims to do."

"Is that why the suicide rate is at an all-time high?"

Doctor Robert paused again, but I didn't desire to spend another minute in his abode, or my plan might be compromised. So I stood up and started to walk out, but not before quipping right in front of his face.

"I've made up my mind. Now you'll have to find someone else to help fund your CD collection."

Exiting his residence, I returned to my car, drove around the block, and parked near the front entrance. I closed my eyes and clenched my fists. I cannot describe the adrenaline I had in that moment, only the satisfaction of yelling "Yes!" The first phase of my plan had succeeded. Now, I just had to wait. Sooner or later, Doctor Robert would leave for work, and that's when I would invade his not-so-humble abode.

CHAPTER 12: AT ETERNITY'S GATE

• • •

After spending a sleepless night in my car, I shut my eyes for a brief moment, but when I opened them, the sunrise was in my eyes, followed by the sight of Doctor Robert driving away. Before exiting my car, I put on gloves, sunglasses, and a hood to protect my identity. I slowly walked over to the front door, constantly looking over my shoulders, ensuring I remained unseen. Despite the grandeur of his residence, security seemed lacking, providing me the opportunity to input the code—1978—and gain entry to another land.

Like a detective at a crime scene, I meticulously explored the doctor's abode, hunting for any sort of hints to the doctor's true nature. I examined many of his possessions, and nothing pointed to anything malicious in his character. Many of these items were things that I would possess, and didn't stand out to me.

I searched room after room after room, always eyeing the clock, making sure I wasn't taking too long, just in case I was forced to bid a hasty retreat. I didn't encounter any elaborate security measures or engage in thrilling action sequences. I wasn't like some roguish scoundrel who planned every detail on a blueprint before committing to this plan. Robert didn't return to the house, and I didn't have to hide in separate rooms to guilefully evade his presence. I didn't use any fancy gadgets to break in. There was nothing theatrical about this; my plan relied on simplicity and originality, unburdened by the need to imitate others.

It then occurred to me that Doctor Robert would probably store his information somewhere. The good doctor was probably not an ultimate criminal mastermind, so he probably stored crucial information in a note-book, due to his love of simpler times. I couldn't believe I was so foolish not to think of this sooner. I quickly walked upstairs, not worrying about any sound I would make; this wasn't a master heist after all. I found his black office space complete with a desk and computer. After searching a drawer or two, I found his handwritten journal. I delved into it, hoping to uncover something useful.

To my surprise, the doctor had a voracious appetite for making notes and journal entries—pages upon pages of writings, some of it dark, some of it light, but most of it hilarious. If he published everything he wrote, he'd sleep on an even bigger pile of money than he currently did. Settling into his office chair, I leaned back, and saw what the good doctor had to say about himself.

PART 3:
THE IMPORTANCE OF
BEING ERNEST

FOR WHOM THE BELL TOLLS

Doctor Robert's Journal: Untitled

In the wee hours of the night, while weary souls were sound asleep, I lay in my bed trying not to weep. And my weeping was always amplified by the intruding thoughts pervading my brain. I lay in my small, dimly lit bedroom, while the moonlight cast eerie shadows on the walls, amplifying the weight of my thoughts and fears. My room was decayed and decrepit, with dirt and grime defacing the walls. Darkness surrounded me like a cloak of shadows. Endless thoughts of fear and dread floated through my mind, making my eyes tired thinking of it, while simultaneously making me too anxious to sleep. Every night I lay under the cold covers of life put upon me by fate, depriving me of vital slumber that would make anyone curl up and cry. I was unable to shut my eyes, and tune out the deafening white noise of my life, or tune out the harrowing memories I experienced day after day. My life resembled a roller coaster ride, with numerous sudden stops and starts. I couldn't remember the last time I was ever happy. In truth, I do not think I ever felt anything other than sadness throughout my whole life.

The earliest memory I can think of was also the most painful memory I can think of, when I was four years old. I had just awoken from a bad dream, and my mom shook me vigorously back and forth to wake me up. She was her usual bedraggled-looking self with her beard and hair. My mom was usually sad and spiteful, but I could tell she was gonna say something important, so I got up and sat on my bed. She looked down for a moment and struggled to articulate the next words that came out of her mouth. The words echoed with such sadness and despair that no human being should ever have the responsibility of saying them.

"Dad passed away last night."

An indescribable pain plagued my brain as soon as she said these words. I was just in shock and couldn't say anything. I was frozen, unable to generate a response.

You see, my dad's dad was a war hero, or at least from my dad's perspective. He served in the 82nd Airborne, specializing in parachute assault operations into enemy territory during WWII. He performed dozens upon dozens of jumps. But one day my grandfather jumped out of a plane and never returned home. His fellow soldiers noticed that he didn't pull his parachute cord, and seemingly committed suicide. However, upon closer inspection, they noticed that he had received multiple gunshot wounds to his heart. For his service, he won the Distinguished Service Cross, among other medals. He lived on his parachute, and died on his parachute.

My dad never really knew his dad. While growing up, his mom just told stories of who he was. These stories fueled my father's curiosity about his dad's heroism and wartime exploits. In his early teens, when he was old enough to form his own thoughts, he aspired to follow in his father's footsteps and become an Airborne soldier. It consumed all of his time, whether it was before, during, or after school. He immersed himself in books about parachute jumping, dedicating himself to physical training through weightlifting and daily runs, preparing himself for the role he longed to embody. He briefly joined the JROTC, but felt disillusioned by those around him, believing they were unworthy of his time and unfit to be true soldiers. So he soon left, married my mom, and I was born shortly after. But his inclination never waned. And a few years after graduating high school and raising me, he could fight the urge no longer, and enlisted in the United States Army's 82nd Airborne division. After completing basic training, he embarked on Jump School to commence his parachute jumps.

However, continuous training took its toll on him, and he soon lost the power to continue training. Day after day, amidst the rigors of military drills, my dad donned his parachute, enduring the exhilaration and euphoria of plummeting through the air. Falling from such heights overloaded his senses, leaving him barely able to deploy the parachute and extricate himself from the dangerous descent. My dad pushed on, as he had to surpass the same sensations his father faced. But he was not his dad, and he grew tired of performing the same task day after day. Still, his drill sergeant drilled into his head that how he felt was of no consequence anymore. And so, one day, my dad practiced another jump, and when he jumped out of the plane, he never pulled his chute. He hurtled towards the earth like a cannonball, and fell flat on the pavement. Upon closer inspection, his superiors noticed that the parachute cord had been severed. They later deemed it an equipment malfunction, as there was no way someone would seemingly commit suicide on a parachute jump. He lived for the parachute, and died on the parachute.

His death was described to my mom in a letter. And that was the last we ever heard from the United States Army. We didn't hear anything from anyone else, as my mom was the only family I had. There was no funeral. There was no spectacle. And there were no tears from heaven running down my face. It was as if I was an island, not involved in the rest of mankind.

I never really knew my dad. As with his dad before him, I just knew stories about him. But even so, I held onto his memory tightly. And I held onto a picture of him even tighter. The picture was my dad in his dark uniform, smiling gracefully. It was a close-up of his face, bathed in a soft and golden light, casting a warm glow over him. I placed it on a dresser near my bed, and I saw it every time I awoke and every time I was about to sleep. I pretended that he was smiling at me. I pretended that he knew me. I pretended that he was always with me. But these were ultimately just pretensions and projections. Without a true family, there was a gaping hole in my life, and my attempt to cherish his memory was an attempt to fill the void. The photograph held a weight that transcended its physical form, and its presence threatened to overwhelm me. I wasn't holding onto a photograph. I was holding onto a piece of him. It was a constant reminder of the aching hole in my life and in my heart. But as I grew in age, I began to doubt the obligation to hold onto memories that were so painful.

The only person left to take care of me was my mom, and she couldn't even take care of herself. I knew my mom, but I never really knew her. She took no interest in anything I did, and I never really had a conversation with her. The only memories I had of her was when she complained about her life, but never did anything to improve it. Based on the bitter whining I heard from her, she bemoaned the decision of marrying my dad straight out of high school. They only dated for a short time and married in an even shorter amount of time. They never learned to communicate with each other or empower each other.

My mom didn't support my dad's decision to join the military and resentment grew between them. My mom wasn't sure of her aspirations and what she wanted in life. She placed that burden on my dad. She expected my dad to take care of her, and so when he began Jump School, and later when he died, she didn't know how to take care of herself. So every week, my mom would bring back a man from the bar and bring him into her bedroom. Every week my mom would buy a bottle of vodka, and every week the alcohol within would be gone. Instead of dismissing her despair, she only desired to diminish her despair. When a new man came home, she'd sometimes mock me and say, "This is your new dad now." And I'd respond that no one could replace my dad. But she drilled into my head that how I felt was of no consequence to her. This was her house, and could rule her house how she chose. Witnessing her repeat the same routine week after week wore me down.

But my mom would grow tired of her boy toys, and desired another kind. I remembered many times when she guided me into her bedroom, laid me down, and put her body all over mine, most of the time without any clothes. She'd kiss me, and she kissed me from head to toe, but mostly on the neck. She'd kiss me on the neck so much that rashes would form there. But the kisses were love for herself, not for me. And when she wasn't kissing, she licked and sucked on places all over my body, whether I was a toddler or a teenager. At the time, someone doing this to me disempowered me. Because she was my mom, she possessed power over me, and so she abused her power to give herself more power. I carried these memories with me throughout my whole life. It evaporated all the love that I could possess for another human being.

As the years stretched into an agonizing eternity, I found myself so impotent that I was engulfed in a suffocating sense of isolation. The weight of my loneliness pressed upon my head, a constant ache that echoed through my very being. My mind lurched with a whirlwind of emotions—a maelstrom of longing, despair, and yearning for connection. I wouldn't wish what I went through on my worst enemy.

While attending public school, I observed my peers engaged in traditional family gatherings, capturing cherished moments in family photos, and embarking on globe-trotting vacations. Among the crowded hallways, I caught glimpses of fleeting interactions, whether it was shared laughter or whispered conversations. Yet, for me, these moments remained distant and elusive. I longed for even the briefest of connections, a chance encounter that would bridge the chasm of my isolation. But I remained invisible, an outsider to the relationships and bonds that seemed to come so effortlessly to others. It was as if I existed in a void, unseen and unheard amidst the bustling world around me. They embraced a communal togetherness, while I remained alone and adrift in a sea of emptiness.

Until one day, I woke up one morning and decided not to be powerless anymore. No event preempted this moment, I just decided not to let external forces dictate my internal thoughts. And the first thing I saw when I woke up was the picture of my dad in his uniform. I picked it up and was conflicted with a whirlwind of emotions. But it soon turned into a whirlwind of anger, when I thought about the powerlessness the photograph put me through, and I slammed it down into a myriad of fragments. I desired to never know this feeling of loss again. I desired to not let my memories overwhelm me. And as soon as that happened, though the hole in my heart remained, it didn't widen.

However, I altered myself in my solitude, and I sought solace and connection with the world in other ways, whether it was through magazines, films, or my favorite: books. Within the pages of books, I discovered a sanctuary—a refuge where I could immerse myself in worlds beyond my own. The classic tales of adventure and the profound wisdom nestled between the lines became a lifeline, guiding me through the labyrinth of my solitude. Each story became a companion, offering solace and a glimpse of a world beyond my own. The dictionary became a daily friend of mine, and I was able to become literate in literary classics by the time I was about to enter high school. In tandem with my intellectual pursuits, I devoted myself to rigorous physical exercise. There would be moments when I was bench pressing, and I couldn't perform another rep. My body would give out and the bar would lie on my chest. There would be no one around to help me, so I eventually figured out that I would place no bench press clips on the bar. And if I failed to do another rep, I would knock the bar to the sides to remove the plates, relieving the weight. Through persistence and countless bench press sessions, my body gradually grew stronger, barely succumbing to exhaustion, and enabling me to consistently complete my reps and sets.

I received no special instruction from my mom, or anyone else on my education or growth. I owed my development entirely to myself. I found the power to do anything I wanted to in life.

End of Entry

THE IDIOT BOY

Doctor Robert's Journal: "Hell"

By the time I was in high school, I was already well-versed in many classics of literature. I delved deeper and deeper into the past, seeking out more challenging works of prose and poetry. Modernist novels and medieval poetry became my fascination, and fortunately my school provided ample time for reading. During lunch periods, I sought solace in the counseling office, the quietest place amidst the normal clamor of the lunchroom. Mindless and boisterous voices overlapped, making it difficult to form a coherent thought without being interrupted by gossip nearby. But it was the normal noise associated with that room, the same thing you'd expect from the shackles of prisoners walking in unison in a chain gang; it was just routine. Nevertheless, reading allowed me to escape the tribulations of the world around me.

You see, I found myself without any friends in high school, not that I desired or needed any. There was nobody in the school worth starting a friendship or relationship with. I possessed enough strength to be alone. The school I attended was a dilapidated institution downtown, a far cry from the quality education I received through private teachings. And the simple reason why is that the faculty and staff seemed disinterested in educating the students, as they themselves lacked a desire for knowledge. It was a common sight to witness teachers engaging in substance abuse with students before the start of each day. Whether it was smoking cigarettes, weed, or experimenting with cocaine, the teachers failed to set a positive example. Instead of being figures the students could aspire to, they were nothing more than replicas of the students they were meant to guide. They were just like everyone else.

Frequent fights erupted in the halls and in classrooms, with no one present to police the situation. I recall one incident where two older male classmates were tormenting a younger student using lacrosse sticks. They relentlessly struck his back while he helplessly stood in a corner of the gym, his eyes closed. He lacked the power to defend himself. It was then that I intervened, using my own lacrosse stick to force them to back off. Ironically, they exclaimed phrases like "Woah, chill man," and "You realize we were just joking," because I guess it wasn't as funny as when I did it.

Such incidents were merely the tip of the iceberg. The school was infested with pseudo-gangs, desperate to portray the image of a gang rather than truly embodying its essence. They reveled in their torn denim clothes, adorned with fake jewelry and numerous piercings. The leader of one of these groups was particularly absurd. He donned a denim jacket with tattered sleeves, his long hair cascading below his shoulders. Three piercings disfigured his face—lip, nose, and eye. Yet none of these organs seemed to be in any use. His appearance was utterly ludicrous, and I wondered how he could face himself in the mirror each day. To make matters worse, his name was Simon. He probably realized how unfit a name Simon was for a gang leader, and he quickly adopted the nickname "The Smasher." How he could say it out loud without anyone laughing was beyond me. Simon took a peculiar interest in me and would tease me whenever he had the opportunity. I retaliated by mocking his name, often referring to him as "The Splinter," which never failed to ignite his fury. I possessed enough power to confront individuals like him.

Eventually, Simon grew bolder. One day, during lunch period, with no one present in the counseling office besides me, Simon and his cronies entered the room, prancing through the double doors like they owned the place. Simon sat directly across from me at the table where I was engrossed in my book, trying to pay no heed to him. He resorted to making faces, clapping, whistling, and trying any number of ways of getting my attention, all to no avail—until he snatched the book out of my hands, and tried reading it with one hand about two feet away from him.

"What you reading, loser?"

"*The Canterbury Tales,* specifically 'The Reeve's Tale.'" Then I whispered, "A reeve's an estate manager."

"Exactly what I'd expect a weirdo like you to be reading. . . . What is this shit anyway?"

I said, "It's medieval poetry, probably way above your feeble mind to comprehend."

"Pfft. Not like any of these words mean anything anyway. It's so old and outdated. You need to get with the times."

"The point of literature is to tell an extraordinary story with ordinary words, so imagine what extraordinary words can do for an extraordinary story."

Simon remarked, "Extraordinary? More like lame! Just try to read some of this guys: 'For levee-fool is with force force of-showvee'?

"'For leveful is with force force of-showve,' or 'It is permissible to repel force with force.' Those annotations at the bottom of the page will help you translate, if you were even smart enough to look at the whole page before reading it, or did your eye piercing get in the way?"

Simon grinned, his eyes filled with malice, as he forcefully slammed the book onto the table.

"Now that's a line of thinking I might actually agree with. . . ."

Simon quickly grabbed the book again, and started forcefully ripping out pages and pages and throwing them in my face, his cronies pointing and laughing. Eventually he ran out of pages, threw what was left on the table, laughed hysterically in my face, and he and his comrades left.

I didn't bother to pick any of it up. I just sighed heavily and rested my head in my hands, debating about what to do next. While moments like these grew more frequent, I always found the strength within to carry on throughout the day.

Looking back on that moment, Simon wasn't the only one who would scoff at what I would read. Classmates at school would lower their eyebrows, or would politely nod or say, "That's cool," but I could see right through them. People say it's difficult to teach a book to yourself. It's not; you just have to be smart about it. You look up words when you don't understand something, and you study criticism from other academics so you can look upon other people's point of view. I was the only one in my whole school who had the power to read such literature.

Speaking of which, I often ignored my classmates and the drama they found themselves in. I preferred to be self-contained, not wanting to engage in any extracurriculars or debauchery that surrounded me. I often overheard about alcohol overdoses, drug overdoses, arrests, vandalism, thefts, assaults, rape, and much more nonsense that went on at our school. I had no sympathy or empathy for those who desired to drag themselves and others into their wretched existence. Not that their presence caused any loss to my situation. I opted for a quiet and peaceful existence away from them, as I rarely found any peace in or out of the classroom.

As I left the classroom that very day, I had barely ventured beyond the school grounds, when a forceful blow struck the back of my head. I fell face-first onto the ground, blood gushing from my nose. Rolling over, I gazed upward, only to hear laughter and taunts as Simon and his henchmen encircled me while I lay flat on the ground, helpless.

"Woohoo, looks like we got the freak now! Oh, what's a matter, Rob? Not so smug now are you?"

He kneeled and got inches from my face, whispering, "You know, that's a really nice leather jacket that you have there. I want it. You don't mind now, do you?"

With blood on my face, I smiled, grabbing my switchblade from my pocket. I pressed the button and the blade emerged like a flash of lightning, and I had just enough force to swipe across his face, wounding him.

Simon staggered on his back in shock, clutching his face, while his companions swiftly kicked the blade away from me and pummeled me further in the face and the torso. I tried shielding myself, but I was over-powered by the force of Simon's minions.

Simon rose to his feet, ordered them to stop, and I caught a glimpse of a prominent red slash across his right cheek. And I couldn't help but smile while I muttered, "Hey, I have a new nickname for you . . . Scarred . . . Scarred Simon . . ."

Then I started laughing.

"Oh funny, funny."

He immediately kicked me in the ribs, and I howled in agony.

"Looks like we have a comedian here. . . . Come on, boys. Let's show Rob here something that's really funny."

And right then, I received the beating of a lifetime. Never before had I received so many forceful kicks to my body. One after the other, kick to the face, the thigh, the ankle, all in rapid succession.

Soon they stopped, and Simon ripped the backpack off my back and poured its contents all over me. Most of it consisted of books. He began to grab novels, hurling them at me one after the other. Then he seized a gigantic textbook, and with all the force he could muster, slammed it against my back.

After that, Simon took all the power he had from me, but he craved more. He grabbed me as I lay on the ground, and tore off my leather jacket. He brazenly donned the jacket and strutted away with his cronies, laughing maniacally.

I rolled over, lying face up, observing the cuts and bruises that cov-ered my arms. I felt my face, and realized I was bleeding profusely from some cuts. But I just didn't care. I just wanted to lie there and not get up. And as I heard Simon's laughter, I just hung my head in agony.

I lay there all alone. No one to help me up. Eventually I did get up, but I was momentarily powerless. I wished someone was there to catch me when I fell. I wished I had any sort of support system to assist me. And then I thought about others who could have been in my situation. And that thought rendered me even more powerless.

At that moment, I wanted no one else to experience what I experienced without help. I wanted to become a psychiatrist. I wanted to become a doctor.

End of Entry

A REEVE'S TALE

Doctor Robert's Journal: "Simon Simmons"

It's unnecessary to recount all the mindless months in my college career. Much of it would bore me to tears if I recounted it. Suffice to say, much of it I don't even remember myself because of how half-witted it was.

To begin, many of my peers were under the influence of drugs and alcohol, a lot of the time at the same time. To most, college was more about learning to ingest as many substances as possible rather than learning anything worthwhile. Consequently, I didn't attend any parties or partake in any extracurriculars. I did at first, but I would frequently engage in imbecilic conversation centered around their sex and drug lives, devoid of any intellectual depth. Harsh as it may sound, many others would likely share the same sentiment, but would acquiesce due to the anxiety of not feeling normal. It was more important conforming to the norm than being anything outside the norm.

But mostly what I learned in school was complete nonsense. The basis for modern psychology was statistics, and the basis for the diagnosis of mental disorders were averages or subjective judgments. This was bluntly hammered into our heads multiple times in many of my courses. "These studies show these types of disorders . . ." They failed to take into account sample size issues, and the multitude of variation within the population. Every rational argument was hitting me with a more precise hammer, demanding me to abandon such a fallacious field.

Yet millions of people flocked to it. Why? It obviously must have helped some people. And if it truly helped people, could I really criticize it?

So I stuck with it. I sunk around ten years of my life into getting my PhD, undergoing foundational/specialty training, and getting licensed until I could finally call myself Doctor Robert Wolfe. But people always called me Doctor Robert as it rolled off the tongue more smoothly.

After all was said and done, I should have been proud of where I ended up. But a tinge of disappointment lingered. The rest of my life would revolve around others overcoming their issues. What about me? Where did I fit in?

This train of thought was not exclusive to me. Year after year, doctors committed suicide, succumbing to the pressures of their positions. And year after year, medical school students superseded them. Many people in this profession felt powerless because of all the despair their patients put them through. As doctors, we were expected to breathe life back into patients, but simultaneously, much of our life was sucked out of us. However, my primary responsibility was to empower those who felt powerless. And that's what has sustained me these past few months, the promise of being a source of support for those who had none. Support I desired, even though I didn't need it.

In college, I was not like most. To balance my studies, I worked all I could in the summertime, then participated in school in the fall and spring. I was able to find jobs that frequently required hard labor, six-ty-hour weeks, seven days a week—an arduous schedule that would break most individuals. But I was immensely rewarded with money to pay for my tuition, my apartment, and all other necessities to survive.

Examining my bank account balance every two weeks filled me with pride. When I was growing up, I wasn't afforded many luxuries besides books due to the low income of my mom. And since I lacked money and all of its benefits growing up, I valued the value of money and discretionary income. The money I earned was the result of labor I exchanged for pay, so I was proud to see how my labor was invested. There were times I partook in a part-time job during school in case my bank account was low, or not high enough. But I easily multitasked even though it wasn't desirable. While literature remained an important hobby, I began to pay more attention to the amount of money I earned summer after summer, always keeping a vigilant eye on my finances.

After years of that routine, and after I fulfilled all my prerequisites to establish my practice, I was able to lease an office in a complex where patients could seek solace. I aimed to create a haven, where my patients could feel safe relieving all their emotions and their worries into one place. I refrained from having my place of business at a residence or my apartment.

I'll leave out all the granular details, but I meticulously designed my office as welcoming as possible, with warm colors and rustic wood furniture to complement it. I designed my own website, espousing my mission of empowering those who felt disempowered. I placed ads online and paid for TV spots. I did anything and everything a self-respecting entrepreneur would do to increase their business. And yet, after a couple of months, not a single patient walked through my doors. As day after day passed, I questioned my career choice, as my bank account balance began to dwindle after each week. I still had more than most, but it wasn't infinite. And eventually, I would run out. I didn't know what I would do without any money.

Then one day I received a call from a man named Mr. Simmons, saying that he wanted to see me. Due to not having clients, I explained that an initial consultation would be expensive, but he interrupted me and stated that he was willing to pay any price. Or maybe it was because he had insurance, and he didn't have to pay any price.

The day came for his session, and I was excited for what would come next. I began to envision changes in my career: lines out the door, patients practically begging to get a session with me. Then, while I was waiting at my desk, about five minutes away from the start of the session, my cell phone rang. The caller ID said "Unknown." I answered it.

"Hello."

"Hello, is this Robert Wolfe?"

"Perhaps, who is this?"

"This is Officer Jenkins with the city police department . . .

The next words that came out of his mouth echoed so halfheartedly that no human being should ever have the responsibility of saying them in such a lifeless manner.

"I'm very sorry to inform you of this, but your mother passed away."

Another indescribable pain plagued my brain as soon as he said these words. I was again in shock, and couldn't say anything as he continued on.

"A neighbor reported a horrible smell coming from inside her house. Once we went in and investigated, we found her body lying on the floor. A doctor performed an autopsy on her and identified alcohol poisoning as the cause of death. But I need you to come down to the station to identify the body."

I still couldn't speak.

"Hello? . . . .Hello? . . . Mr. Wolfe?"

And then I hung up. My mother and I were always distant towards each other. She was barely even a parent, as I took care of myself more than she did me. I had to get a job to put food on the table. I didn't receive any gifts from her for my birthdays or any other holidays. I wouldn't get any support from her whatsoever. The only thing she provided was a roof over my head—a fact she always loved to throw in my face, an excuse that terrible parents use to justify their power.

But she didn't have friends, or any other family besides my dad. The only thing she did was drink alcohol and watch TV. But as soon as I heard that news, it felt like life was on pause. The news zapped my strength from me. It seemed that everything around me stopped moving.

But it didn't. I checked the clock and it was time for my session. I stood, tried to shrug off the news, and trudged towards the room.

Mr. Simmons was pacing in the room, constantly twitching and looking over his shoulder, as if he was afraid of his own shadow. As soon as I entered, I straightened up and greeted him.

"Hello, Mr. Simmons."

He abruptly stopped in his tracks, and attempted to meet my gaze. His head hung low, hands clasped together, and he struggled to form words as he responded.

"Hello . . . You . . . You can . . . You can call me . . . Simon."

Simon. The name carried a bitter distaste of someone from my past. He looked vaguely similar to him. He had scars all over his face, mostly holes from where piercings probably were. However, he had a beard, short hair, and many facial blemishes, such as wrinkles and moles. This combined with his timid behavior and the vast unlikelihood of him seeking me out made me realize it wasn't the same Simon.

Nevertheless, I tried continuing the conversation. And just from a quick look, Simon Simmons looked like a poor sad sack who needed some therapy. Simon Simmons. What a ridiculous name. He was probably bullied in high school.

"Well, Simon . . . my name is Doctor Robert Wolfe. Please come into my office and we can begin our session."

I confidently began to walk to my office and looked back to see that Simon was still standing there.

"Well, come on," I said, and he finally followed with heavy steps. Seeing such a sad sack put on such a timid display briefly made me forget about the heartbreaking news I had received. It gave me power.

I strutted into my office and had a seat. Simon trudged in and collapsed into my special therapist chair. Before speaking, I had him sit there for about a minute, gauging him. I prepared a clipboard and a notepad, ready to take notes. It was clear something was wrong just from his body language, and how he kept twitching around in his surroundings. He was scared to divulge his difficulties but was anxious to share them with me. And it shouldn't have been too difficult to pry from him.

"So Simon, how are you feeling?"

"I'm fine."

That clearly wasn't true. I decided to have some fun and incorporated a charming tone to deliver my clichéd lines out of the psychiatrist handbook. I used all my effort not to laugh while reciting them.

"Simon, you don't have to lie anymore. This is a safe haven for all your thoughts. You can talk to me. I won't judge you."

There was silence from Simon when I uttered those words. He began to say something, then quickly stopped himself. He tried to say something again, his perturbed countenance betraying his struggle to articulate his thoughts. And then he finally found his voice.

"No, I'm not fine."

"And why is that Simon? What's wrong?"

"Robert, I don't know. I just feel sad. I can't explain it. It's just when I'm going through my day, I get sad. Really sad, for no reason. It just comes out of nowhere. When I'm going through my day, I feel like curling up on the ground and crying just to make the pain stop. This happens almost every day. I want it to stop. But it's just a pain that plagues my brain constantly. I just wish it wouldn't come at all."

"And why do you think you feel sad, Simon?"

"I just can't stop thinking about memories from high school, and how I was endlessly bullied and tortured. Every day I was exposed to the worst humanity has to offer."

Hmph. Sounds like something I would say.

"You see, crime was common in the area I grew up. Many kids my age were poor, and turned to crime to . . . to . . ."

"Regain the power in their lives?"

"Yes, exactly. And what made this worse were the gangs. In order to fit in and protect yourself, you had to join a gang. And many did, to imitate those around them. When you were a member, people would think twice about messing with you. To stand up to them, I made my own gang. . . ."

No, it can't be. . . .

"They called me Simon the Smasher, as I had a reputation of fighting, and winning those fights. You could call me one of the local heroes of the school. People looked up to me, and I would frequently try to help others who were bullied by the gangs."

His words were nothing more than a web of lies. He didn't even remember me, even though I was his prime target on many occasions. He wasn't even taken seriously by any of the bigger gangs, and would frequently lose fights to them. To make up for his frustration, he would take out his anger on people who weren't in gangs. People like me.

"This all sounds great, Simon. But you wouldn't be coming to me if everything were great. So why are we here? Why do you feel sad?"

"Well, you see, Doctor, it's because of all this trauma I went through. It makes me feel powerless. I can't get it out of my head."

"What trauma? Can you be more specific?"

"Well, you see . . ."

And then I zoned out. I pretended to listen to what he was saying. Then I took my clipboard in my hand, changed my sitting position, and wrote some nonsensical scribbles on my piece of paper.

He just kept blabbering on and on about how hard his life was, and how his experiences affected him today. Except these experiences were fabricated. Never before have I seen a man so dissociated from reality. He just couldn't stop talking about himself. He kept using the word "hero" so repetitively that I can't even begin to describe it; it would fail to capture the absurdity that I was witnessing.

"Simon," I interrupted him, as this uninterrupted soliloquy wasn't getting anywhere.

"Did you ever hurt anyone in high school?"

"What?"

"Did you ever hurt anyone? You said you were in a gang, so you must have hurt people who didn't deserve it?"

"Everyone I hurt deserved it."

"Everyone?"

"Everyone. They would smash me like a bug. But nothing gives me greater satisfaction than putting a bully in their place."

I couldn't agree more, Simon.

"I thought you said many times you were a local hero and tried to look after your classmates."

"Oh yes, yes. That too. Of course."

"Right."

I continued to doodle on my clipboard.

He had to die. Simon must die. Simon was experiencing the same loneliness I experienced in high school, but now it looked as though he had nobody left to rely on, nobody left to believe his lies. He was on his knees, begging for me to help him. He was so self-absorbed, he couldn't even remember me, or even my face. I wondered how many people he hurt that he couldn't remember as well. I had nothing. I HAD NOTHING! And now he was acting like he was a victim, like he was the hero of a fairy tale. But now he didn't have the same power as he once did, and was under my thumb, rather than the other way around. Simon needed a savior right now; Simon needed a doctor. But I didn't feel like saving him at all. In fact, I was going to do everything I can to kill him.

I looked up from my scribbling, "Simon, I'm going to do everything I can to help you. From what you've told me, I'm diagnosing you with clinical depression, as these episodes you're experiencing detail a persistent depression that won't go away without medical intervention. There is a poor prognosis for this disease, as these symptoms you're feeling will continue to worsen without my help. But with my help, you will feel better and faster than you ever could on your own. I know specific treatments that will put you in the peak of health. You couldn't be in safer hands."

"Thank you so much, Robert. It already feels like a massive weight has been lifted off my shoulders."

This fool has already sealed his fate. He knew nothing about mental illness, how it was diagnosed, and how it was treated, which made him gullible enough to kill. Many people didn't educate themselves on psychology, and didn't understand that the power of what you're diagnosed with is ultimately in my hands, not in anything scientific. There was no special test for depression, or any other mental disorder. It was based primarily on a checklist assigned by the DSM-5 handbook, where you'll find only about 100% of those symptoms were subjective judgments. Symptoms were byproducts after discovering a disease, and should not be used as criteria to diagnose someone. To put it simply, you could have symptoms for the flu and not have the flu. But people were so gullible, like Mr. Smasher here, that they willingly gave up all their power and trusted every word that came out of my mouth simply because I had a doctorate degree. But Mr. Smasher didn't need to know that.

Dealing with trauma is never an easy process. But Simon probably expected to walk in here, and make me give him some magic pill that would automatically make him feel better. And I did possess some; I'd make him end his pain very swiftly.

"Simon, I'm prescribing you two medications. One is called citalopram, which you need to take twice a day, and the other, isocarboxazid, which you need to take four times a day. Now the pharmacy may refuse your medications, but just tell them to call me and I will take care of it. Your depression is so severe that it needs immediate and potent medicine to combat it. It's the only way to help your condition."

"Okay."

Simon, I'm prescribing you mind-altering drugs that scientists don't know much about that will likely cause extreme symptoms that will have you begging on your knees in pain, due to a theory that has long since been discredited.

"I will do what you ask, Doctor."

Unluckily for him, these medications when combined will erratically alter his serotonin levels, which will cause serotonin syndrome. It will increase his heart rate, blood pressure, and blood temperature, which will cause insomnia, agitation, headaches, seizures, hypomania, and even hallucinations. The agony from these side effects will be boundless, and if he reports these side effects to me, all I have to say is that these afflictions will subside and are due to his depression. But he won't believe me, and will resort to the most common at home pain remedy available: a magic bullet, a single slug straight to the head. Which will give me what I always wanted, to see that brainless, pig-headed bully bite the dust.

As I suspected, and as the months passed by, his symptoms began to worsen, and he kept prattling to me about how painful it was. I began to figure out that the more I told him to come and see me, the more money I would receive. So I found ways to keep him coming back, and kept diagnosing him with other disorders, which led to more sessions, which led to more prescribed medicine, which led to me getting paid more.

The key to being a doctor was that the cure is the disease. It wasn't really in my best interest to help anybody, then people would never come back to me. So I had to produce problems in order to solve them, which wasn't difficult to do. The main problem in this world was our fixation with trying to solve a problem that wasn't there. But people would rather not take responsibility to try and make their lives better. They'd rather pay me money and give me the responsibility. With that responsibility, I created complications. And those complications brought the pleasure of seeing my bank account numbers rise.

But there was another pleasure that commenced. And it began with one of my last sessions with Simon.

Simon remained in the waiting room as usual, and at our session time, I strutted over to get him. As he was sitting down, he kept fidgeting in his seat. His twitching had gotten worse over the past couple of months, but now it was as if he was performing a dance move every five seconds. I greeted him and he followed me back to my office, where we began our session.

"So, Simon, how is everything?"

"It's terrible, Doc. I still feel sad. I've been having headaches all the time, trouble sleeping . . . I just feel so horrible."

"Have you been taking your meds?"

"Yes."

"Then you should have nothing to worry about. The symptoms you're experiencing are tied to your depression, and will fade away."

He replied, "These symptoms didn't start until I started taking the medication. Can you explain that?"

"Obviously, these medications you've been taking have side effects. I can't think of a single drug that has zero side effects. But as I said, these symptoms are more likely coming from your depression."

"How?"

"Well, Simon, depression is a very complex disorder. . . ."

No, it's not.

"What affects it is your genetics, environment, and many other factors. . . ."

No, it doesn't work like that.

"But a lot of it is your mentality, how you're responding to your stimuli . . ."

That's all it is.

"So there must be something you haven't told me yet, something deep inside, some unsaid trauma that is causing this reaction."

Take the bait. Take the bait.

"Well, to tell you the truth doctor . . . I'm not a hero. . . ."

I know.

"I hurt a lot of people in high school. I was a bully. My gang wasn't really a gang, and I went around hurting people because it made me feel good. It gave me purpose."

He then started crying and put his head in his hands. I offered him my tissues.

How pathetic. I won't let his tears dissuade me now. All I wanted was him six feet dead in the ground.

"Simon, what reason is there to live by being a bully?"

"What?"

"What reason is there to live by lying about your past?"

"I . . . don't know."

"I want you to go home and think about your life. I want you to think about all the harm that you've caused. And I want you to ask your-self, 'What reason is there to keep me waking up in the morning?'"

"Okay."

And then I cut the session short, and he stormed out. But he still paid me for the full session. A better man might have put two and two together to realize that I was causing his torment, or change his life around. But he was a lesser man, and I knew exactly where his life was headed as soon as he left the room.

A few days later, Simon killed himself. He shot himself straight in the head and blew whatever life he had left in him out with his brains.

And that wasn't even the best part, Simon was so deep under my thumb that he had recommended other people to me, and I was able to sustain an income. Soon, those people recommended others, and those others recommended others, and so on and so forth. Word of mouth grew, and my website began to get hits, and received good reviews from review websites. It took a while, but I became quite an established doctor.

CHAPTER 15: A REEVE'S TALE

At this point in time, I had felt more power than any other part of my life.

End of Entry

UNDER MY THUMB

Doctor Robert's Journal: "Lauro Ricketts"

"Doctor, I have never felt more powerless than any other time in my life."

"Well, Vincent, after having many sessions with you, I know what the problem is."

"You do?"

"Yes, you suffer from . . ."

What should I say this time? Intermittent explosive disorder? ADHD? Oh, I know!

"Bipolar disorder."

"Bipolar?"

"Yes, bipolar. You frequently experience intense mood swings, combining explosive bouts of anger with implosive bouts of depression. The answer is clear."

"I do not suffer from bouts of anger!" he angrily retorted to me after rising up from his chair.

"Clearly."

After yelling at me, he slowly sank back down to his chair. Then he pathetically started to cry. I simultaneously acted concerned while keeping my eye on the clock behind him, waiting for the session to be over. Seconds remained, and Vincent still continued to cry. Then, barely able to form syllables, he began to speak.

"Doc-Doctor . . . I . . . I . . ."

It was now a minute after the session was supposed to end, and this wasn't going anywhere. So, I ended the session. I wasn't being paid overtime anyway.

"Yes, yes. This is obviously distressing news for you, Vincent. I can see you need some time to process this. So think it over, and we'll address it in our next session. In the meantime, I'll prescribe you some medication so you can deal with these episodes. But remember to take your medicine. That's the most important part. Remember to take your medicine. . . ."

So it makes you think I'm actually helping you. So you can keep coming back to me for more prescriptions. So I can get more power.

". . . So you can get more power."

"Th-thank you, Doctor."

And then he finally got up and trudged away from my office.

I swore an oath in graduate school to provide superlative treatment to all of my patients. Yet I more or less spent years through endless university classes as a promise to earn a six-figure income. But the elevated amount of money on my paychecks were in inverse proportion to my satisfaction. I sat in tedium with patients who whined about their problems incessantly. And if there were no problems for me to solve, I didn't get paid.

I discovered it was more advantageous to generate issues rather than resolve them upon arrival. Most of my patients' issues could have been solved through self-reflection, but all of them lacked the willpower to do so on their own. Most even seemed happier. It was a placebo; the more I told them I was working through their problems, the more they believed it, and the more I got paid.

It always came back to that for me: money. When I looked at a patient, I didn't see a human being, I saw a business transaction. You could call me a businessman more than a doctor. I didn't really use any science in my day-to-day life anyway.

As a matter of fact, it was around this time that I was yearning for even more money. You see, money was like sex, once you start getting it, you just desire more and more of it. And there's nothing wrong with that. You can never have enough money.

And I saw a money-making machine walk straight through my door.

"Hello, Doctor Robert?"

"Hello, Mr. Ricketts. Please sit."

The boy before me looked incredibly skinny, yet he was wearing a red high school football jersey, along with a cast on his arm, so I decided to comment on this.

"Nice jersey. You play football, I assume?"

"Oh, I'm the MVP for the team."

"Are you? What position do you play?"

He answered, "I'm a receiver. I score points for the team."

"Other players can do that, can't they?"

"My coach wants to protect the quarterback, so he makes us pass a lot of the time, and as a result, I score lots of points."

"But you obviously don't now, due to your injury, correct?"

He scoffed, raised his cast to look at it, then continued.

"This is just a sprain. I should be back in a couple weeks."

"Well then, Lauro, what brings you to my office today? What problem are you trying to solve?"

"I don't know, I just feel sad. I can't explain it. It's just when I'm going through my day, I get sad. Really sad, for no reason. It just comes out of . . ."

I'd heard this before almost a million times. I just doodled on my clipboard until he stopped talking.

". . . I just wish it wouldn't come at all."

Okay, let's see. What drugs should I recommend this time? Adderall, Prozac, uhh. Oh wait, money machine, I was so bored I almost forgot. I addressed his concerns first.

"And why do you feel sad, Lauro?"

"Because I feel like a failure."

Maybe because you are.

"No, you're not. You clearly have an important role for the team. How could you say that?"

He explained, "Because in practice, I don't really play that hard. I don't really study our football plays. None of my other team members do it, it's super hard, and I'm too busy to find time for it, so I don't really have any motivation to do it. And I don't really care about winning a game."

"Then why do you play?"

"To make it seem . . . I mean, to be important."

What a loser. This shouldn't be difficult at all.

"Then the problem is clear, Lauro."

"It is?"

You're a poor, sad, nobody who's unhappy imitating everyone else, but has no willpower to try and do anything else. It's a common condition.

"Yes. You're suffering from anxiety from trying to follow existing social cues and rules. It's a common condition."

"Wow. Really? I haven't thought of it like that."

It was always amusing that I was able to solve people's problems within five minutes of them telling it to me, but again, I'd be out of a job if that was the case, so I had to keep them coming back.

"I'm diagnosing you with . . .

Is it GAB, or is it GLAD? No, wait.

"GAD."

There's so many meaningless mental disorder titles that even I have trouble keeping track of them.

"Or generalized anxiety disorder. This disorder causes unrealistic desire and fear about your everyday life. But it will not cease, and will require extensive sessions in order to fully address it. You can expect to come here almost every week."

"Why is that necessary?"

I responded, "You explained yourself that you experience anxiety daily, and as such will need assistance often in order to fully address the anxiety and make sure it doesn't overwhelm you."

"But why do I need you for that?"

Ahh, sometimes I receive pushback, but it's easily countered.

"You don't need me at all. You don't ever have to use my services. But I am trained to deal with disorders like yours, and possess certain techniques to tackle your disorder and train you to deal with it. You can leave whenever you wish. But I'm willing to bet that since you came here, you would like to make use of what I can offer."

"It's just, that's gonna take so much time out of my week. I wish there was a simpler solution."

Got him.

"Well, there is one, possibly."

"There is?"

"Yes, but it's not necessarily for everyone."

Lauro begged with sadness in his eyes, "Tell me, please."

"A popular method of treating anxiety is the use of medications. The one I often recommend is estazolam, which will make the neurotransmitters less active in your body, and loosen anxiety's hold on your mind."

Did I mention it is also highly addictive and can cause withdrawal if not taken constantly?

"But just because you're having a really bad day doesn't mean you qualify for the drug."

"But it's not just today, it's every day, doctor. Will it make my problems go away?"

No. That power is in your hands.

"Yes. That power is in my hands. I will prescribe you the drug. But I still recommend sessions so I can keep track of your progress."

. . . So I can further break you under my thumb.

A couple of months passed. I won't dwell on all the tedious sessions I endured with Mr. Rickets, as much of it mirrored the routine experiences I had with many of my patients. He complained about his problems, and I, in turn, feigned attentive concern. I was probably the only one in his life who cared to listen. Truth be told, I didn't really care and I didn't really listen. But I could keep pretending as long as he kept paying me.

I readied myself for another session with Mr. Rickets, when a sudden knock on the door interrupted my preparations. I rose, walked over, and opened the door. Before me stood Mr. Rickets, fully living up to his name. I ushered him in as he walked into the room, or should I say hobbled into the room. His arm was no longer in a cast, but now his left leg was encased, and he struggled with his crutches for a minute before finally settling into the therapist's chair.

"Hello, Lauro, how's high school football going?"

"What does it look like? I got injured on the first play of the first game and I'm out for the season."

Saw that coming a mile away.

"Wow, who could have seen that coming?"

"I know."

"How does that make you feel?"

"I feel like a failure. I don't know if I've told you that."

You have. You tell me that every session. God only knows how many more times you'll tell me.

"But my teammates don't even want to talk with me anymore. In fact, they call me names, like Rickets or Lauro the Loser. And even when they don't, I hear about them constantly gossiping about me. . . ."

He looked down, and seemed like he was about to shed a tear, but refrained from doing so.

"That's awful. I can't imagine anyone who could do such a thing."

Then he stopped refraining and began to cry in front of me. Out of tiresome instinct, I handed him my tissue box and he took some out.

"Sometimes when I'm alone, I just go to the school bathroom and cry. It just feels like the whole world can't imagine what I'm going through."

"Oh, I don't think you're alone at all, Lauro. In fact, I'm willing to bet many of your peers experience the same thing you do, but they belittle those they can find fault with in order to feel empowered. You see, we're all exercising in a prison of our own construction, and many aren't able to break free."

"How can one break free, Doctor?"

I responded, "By going to therapy, of course."

"Do you think everyone should go to therapy?"

Yes. I benefit from it a lot with little to no effort.

"Yes. Everyone can benefit from a licensed professional who uses science to understand human behavior and human's plights."

A few seconds passed, with obvious facial expressions of discontent and disagreement.

"Lauro, how do your parents feel about you attending therapy?"

"They're the ones who recommended me coming here."

"Why?" I asked.

"Because . . . because . . . they believe I can benefit from psychiatric help."

"Lauro, that's not it, is it?"

"No . . . it's because they don't want to listen to my problems."

"Lauro?"

"It's because they think something's wrong with me. It's because I don't act like them."

Then he began to cry more and seized a handful of tissues.

This was a common experience I heard from many of my patients. With the emerging popularity of psychology, many parents referred their children to psychological help because they didn't want to invest the time and effort to provide support or to communicate with them. The human population boasted immense diversity, and therefore a great diversity of expression, emotional responses, and so on. But parents nowadays worried that every slight variation of behavioral difference was a sign of mental illness. But I didn't mind; I got paid more.

"Well, Lauro, it's important to recognize social cues and possess the ability to communicate with those around you. It doesn't mean they think something's wrong with you."

Well, that was a complete lie. No one recommends someone to a doctor if nothing is wrong. A doctor was someone who could fix problems, except for me. But he didn't need to know that.

"Sometimes I wish I didn't have to fit in. It's just so exhausting. Speaking of which, can you renew the prescription for my meds? I'm almost out."

I think it's time to enact stage two of my plan.

"Well, Lauro, it's important to pace yourself. I'm not sure another prescription is necessary right now."

"BUT I NEED IT!"

And then he cried more and more, grabbing more tissues, until there were no more in the box. He was hooked, just like I planned.

"Well, tell you what, Lauro. I'm going to prescribe you double the usual. But I want you to get it filled, then sell it to your friends, and bring me half of what you make off of it."

"What? Won't that be illegal?"

"Very. But everyone breaks the law at some point in their lives, and you mentioned you wanted to fit in, correct? Breaking the law doesn't necessarily equate to committing an immoral act. And if you want to avoid getting caught, you have to keep it just small enough, and then the law won't be breathing down your neck. So I recommend selling it to a few high school classmates."

"But I don't want to get caught."

I explained, "The pharmaceutical industry's net worth exceeds a little more than a trillion dollars. Many people informally sell pharmaceutical drugs, because everyone uses pharmaceutical drugs, and not everyone wants to go see a psychiatrist to get a prescription for it. No one will want to turn you in, because everyone uses it. And from what you've told me, it sounds like your classmates purchase a variety of other drugs anyway. However, it is wise to be cautious. To be safe, I recommend only selling to those who you know use other types of drugs."

"But what about my parents?"

"What about them?"

"Aren't they obligated to know everything we've been discussing? Won't they find out?"

I stated, "Your parents have signed my confidentiality agreement. I am allowed to tell them as little or as much as I want. I can't hide everything, but anything incriminating won't be found out by them. Your parents have to be involved to pick up the prescriptions, and I can easily make up reasons, such as 'Lauro is feeling down and needs the extra medication.'"

"Won't the pharmacists get suspicious?"

"No, trust me. They won't."

Because they were like me. They didn't get paid if they didn't provide. And pharmaceutical companies compensated me every time I prescribed medication. The key thing to remember was that these companies weren't concerned with helping people work through their problems. They were a business. They were manufacturers of products, and they wanted their products sold. Because of the Physician Payments Sunshine Act, any payment from the pharmaceutical companies to me had to be reported. But that meant nothing. The pharmaceutical drug market was such a money maker that there was too much data to track and analyze on where it was going, or at least assume that the data was criminal behavior. It was why I prescribed so much medication—the pharmaceutical companies wanted to reward me for assisting in selling their product. Now, as I said, if you accepted too much, you painted a target on your back. But so much medication is passed around nowadays, it wasn't too much of a concern. Lauro might run out of refills, but again, I could easily make up reasons so he wouldn't run out.

"I don't know. . . ."

"Lauro, if you do this, you'll be the hero on campus. Everyone will look up to you and come to you for help. You will be helping them. Many other students your age face anxiety all the time, and you will be providing them a way to cope with that. The bullying will stop, and you will achieve your dream of fitting in. You will empower them and you will empower yourself."

"Yes, yes . . ."

Yes, yes.

Many months and many sessions passed. Lauro kept giving me a cut for all the prescriptions that he sold, and I was receiving money from the pharmaceutical companies for prescribing the medication. It wasn't much, but that small amount of money paid for some of my necessities, and my plan would provide even more money down the line. Yet money wasn't entirely the reason. At first it was, but I began to take pleasure from having him under my thumb, and it became the motivating force for me to continue what I was doing, despite the risk. And for once, Lauro appeared in my room without any casts or any sprained limbs. He sat comfortably in my chair.

"Doctor, I want to start today . . . I don't feel like a failure anymore. These past months, I've done what you asked and I feel like I fit in. As you know, I've sold those medications you've prescribed me, and my classmates have started to like me."

It wasn't that they liked you. It was because of what you can provide for them.

"I have friends, I even have a girlfriend . . . just, life is good."

"That's great to hear. Since everything is going well, it's probably best if you don't sell those medications anymore. I don't want to . . . I don't want you to get caught, and as I said, you have to keep it small enough in order to get away with breaking the law."

"But what about them getting more medications?"

I smiled. "Just recommend them to me, and I'll be happy to prescribe them, if they qualify for it."

More patients just like that. All part of the plan.

"Makes sense. I might even recommend my girlfriend to you if that's alright. I might wait a while until the right time, but I think she can really benefit from a doctor like you. But I did want to tell you something else."

"Yes?"

"I don't want to be your patient anymore. I'm in a good position right now, and I don't want to see you anymore."

I fake smiled.

"Of course. You are free to leave whenever you feel like it."

He smiled, rose from his chair, and shook my hand.

"Wow. Thanks. You took that better than I thought. You're the best, and I appreciate everything you've done for me."

"Of course. Feel free to come back anytime if you need anything."

He smiled again, and walked out. And I knew he'd come back. He might come back in a few weeks, or maybe a month. Because either he'd be in withdrawal and need someone to prescribe medications, or he'd face another problem he couldn't solve and wouldn't be able to ask his parents or those around him, because they wouldn't care. He could go to another doctor, or find some other way to get medications, but he was probably not smart enough to consider that. He'd be forced to come back to the one person who would listen to him—me.

I enjoyed having him under my thumb. It gave me power. Maybe a few years down the line, I'd produce another complication and prescribe him opioids or something like that. It wouldn't mix well with the current medication and the other drugs and alcohol that he'd likely take in college. I'd hear in the news about the overdose of a boy in college. The idea that his life was in my hands brought a genuine smile to my face.

Most of the world wouldn't take notice, but the few who did would have the memory erased when something else popped up that gave them something to converse about. And I could move on to the next patient who I could put under my thumb.

End of Entry

17.

LOLITA

Doctor Robert's Journal: "Maddy Phrey"

Time continued to pass, and money had become an abundant burden. I purchased a half-million-dollar home, replete with my own library of books and music. My expenses knew no bounds, yet my desires were modest. Dining out became an exercise in ignorance of the bill, and subscriptions were acquired without the slightest concern for cost. Money, once an ever-looming concern, had transformed into a trivial afterthought.

One of the key things I was most proud of was remodeling my office. I made the office as foreboding as possible to catch my patients off-guard. Sometimes I would make patients languish in the waiting room, forced to confront the stark white walls. I emphasized whiteness with minimal decorations, so it made my patients not focus on anything external. It made them think internally about their life. It made them mentally prepare for my session. It worked brilliantly. Most people didn't reflect or think internally, and this would force them too. It would bring to light painful memories for them before a session, convincing them that they needed my services even more. My office would then psychologically become a space for people to reflect. I was asking them to come back without even having to ask.

I'm a man who didn't want to rest on his laurels, or didn't rest at all. As such, I decided to turn inward a little more, and focus more on personal development. As previously stated, I always thought it was important to stay in shape. I exercised routinely, but didn't have full access to all the equipment I could have at the gym, so I expanded my horizons and exercised at the gym more often than at home.

A few months passed, I proudly noticed there was this girl who kept checking me out at the gym. It always gave me warm satisfaction and amusement, as I would frequently catch her staring in the gym mirror, or I would glance over at her and she would quickly look away. She was a tall girl, and very voluptuous. She was well-proportioned in all aspects of her body, boasting long and thick raven hair to top it off. I admired that I had a secret admirer.

I could explain further. But in truth, I just wanted to fuck her at first sight, last sight, or any other time she was in my sight.

A few months later, I decided to make a move. Some people over-complicate this step, and another version of myself might have, but it wasn't difficult at all. What I'm about to explain was the first of many interactions I've had with the opposite sex. You could say it was the turning point of gaining even more power.

You see, the goal of any interaction with a female was to get her to say yes. And how did I make her say yes? By taking charge and convincing her that was what she wanted. By thinking of "What's in it for her?" I made myself appear like it was what she wanted, but didn't actually have to.

Case in point, I had to place abstract values concretely into conversation. For example, I exemplified charm and interpolated that in my speech. It wasn't something that could be taught, only learned. But I also made conversations flow naturally, and concealed my intentions; otherwise there was no chase, and there was fun in the chase.

I walked up to this lonely girl, who was resting near a squat rack.

"Hello, Miss Sunshine, I couldn't help but notice that you were squatting some pretty heavy weight there, and I was wondering if you need a spotter or a knight in shining armor to make sure you don't die?"

"Haha. No thanks. I appreciate the offer though."

It was important not to panic when brushed off. What a girl says she wants and what she actually wants are two different things.

"Haha. Okay, maybe you don't need a knight in shining armor, but joking aside, you have three plates on this bar. That's a lot of weight; that's 315 pounds. I'd recommend a spotter to make sure you don't injure yourself. Even I use spotters."

"Haha. Well, okay."

A few seconds passed, and she explained that she was aiming for five reps. She got under the bar, breathed, and then lifted the bar with all her might. I was right behind her, not touching her, but squatting with her just in case she failed. But she didn't. She squatted five reps in perfect form with no assistance.

She put the bar back on the rack. "Told you I didn't need a spotter."

"I stand corrected. May I ask the name of my fellow champion?"

"Ashley."

"Good to meet you, Ashley. My name's Robert. But most call me Doctor Robert, as I am their psychiatrist."

"A psychiatrist?"

"Yes. I get paid to listen to people prattle on about their problems eight hours a day, five days a week. . . .?

I also love fucking with my patients.

"Or sorry, what I meant to say was that I have a passionate desire to help people through their problems, and I also support world hunger and whatever cause you care about."

She burst out laughing as she walked up to the bar.

She lifted the bar and I was squatting with her as she lifted it. She had more difficulty lifting the weight this time, as she kept laughing and had trouble keeping the bar parallel. But as she struggled lifting, I kept encouraging her by saying, "You can do it!" or "Come on, you got it!" I noticed during the last rep that she pressed her ass up against my crotch and stayed there for a few seconds until she finally put the bar back on the rack.

"Tell me, Doctor, are you looking for new patients?"

I smiled, "Well . . . it would depend on the patient."

She whispered in my ear, "How about a bad little girl who's looking for another daddy to punish her?"

I whispered back, "I think that's right up my alley, for the right price."

She walked backwards, turned around to the bar, got underneath, then quickly backed out, turned back around to me, and said, "Want to get out of here? I can think of some other exercises we can do at my place."

I don't think I need to explain what happened afterwards at her apartment. Just imagine the most stimulating sensation you've ever experienced and multiply that by one hundred.

But I will explain what happened with Ashley afterwards. It turned out that Ashley told the truth in that little whisper. She was a daddy's girl, though I didn't know why. She explained to me that her father sexually abused her as a child, taking a heavy toll on all aspects of her life. She described the anxiety that traumatic event caused her, making it difficult to form attachments with others. Yet despite the abuse, she developed a fondness for sex, and being abused during sex. I learned all of this because she became my patient soon after. I prescribed her clonazepam, a medication used to treat anxiety, but which also caused drowsiness, memory problems, and confusion. You could say that placed her under my thumb.

And she wanted to stay there, as she begged to stay around me as much as possible. I offered her a job as my secretary, as it was getting difficult to do all this administrative work without any assistance. But mainly it was nice to have a little fun when patients weren't around, whether it was in the morning, between sessions, after closing, or all of the above. I bet she thought she was repaying me for everything I'd done for her, but really she only existed for my pleasure.

There were rules that psychiatrists could never practice on anyone they loved. But I never was big on following rules, nor did I love anyone.

Soon after, I received a call from Lauro stating that his girlfriend, Maddy, was coming to see me.

She came through the door of my office, and I was quite mesmerized by how she looked. She didn't look like she had the body of a teenager; she seemed to possess a much older build. I don't feel the need to describe how she looked, as she looked breathtaking. All I need to say is that she started a fire in my loins as soon as she walked in.

I stood up and reached out my hand. She waited a few seconds, but then eventually shook my hand. But in those few seconds, she licked her lips and dilated her pupils. It seems my loins weren't the only ones that were turned on.

"You must be Maddy. Lauro has said so much about you, but I'm afraid I'm not allowed to share it."

She laughed and then sat down in my therapist chair.

"That bodes well, so I know that everything I share with you is purely confidential."

Well, actually, it isn't. Anyone with subpoena power had access to my records, which nowadays was everyone. I never put anything incriminating in my official records, but I had to possess some notes in case I was ever asked about a patient. Health insurance companies were a good example. They were paying for the treatments, so they wanted to know about what was transpiring. They rarely ever went against anything I performed, but they received information about the patients nonetheless. I communicated with them on a consistent basis, and once I shared it with them, who knows what people intercepted that information. Many people think that my patients' notes were locked away in vaults, never heard from again, because people were content in believing in myth and imitating that myth.

"I assure you, anything you say will be locked away in a vault, never heard from again. This is a safe space for your thoughts."

But mostly my thoughts.

"Well, Doctor, this is the part where I say how sad I feel all the time."

If only you knew how true that was . . .

"And it is true, Doctor. But the reason for it is different than most. . . ."

She looked down and seemed like she was about to cry, and as a reflex I began to hand her the tissues. But she just closed her eyes, took a deep breath, and swatted them away. Incredible.

"It's just . . . I don't feel like I have an identity. I'm under pressure from my friends to fit in. I'm under pressure from my parents to over-achieve in my grades. And I'm under pressure from Lauro to be a sup-portive girlfriend. From every angle, someone is telling me who I should be, besides me. Most of the time I'm able to shrug it off. But it's all just adding up like bricks in a wall. As such, it really gives me a strong passion for female empowerment, but . . ."

You just really want to empower yourself.

"I just really want to empower myself."

As usual, I was doodling in my notepad. But I also felt engrossed in every word she was saying. She wasn't my usual patient. She seemed to have a clear understanding of her problem. So I wondered why she was coming to see me.

"Well, Maddy, it seems you've made my job very easy. So then that makes me wonder why you've come to see me."

"Because I was recommended to, by my parents, by my friends, by Lauro."

Hmmm. It seems I caught Miss Perfect in a moment of vulnerability, and I intended to exploit that vulnerability to the fullest potential.

"Well, Maddy, I want to make sure that I'm not leaving anything unaccounted for. It's easy for any one of us to get bottled up. But again, this is a safe space, and I want to ask you, is there anything that you want to share that you haven't shared with anyone?"

She looked down and remained silent.

"Anything at all?"

"Nothing, Doctor."

"Nothing, huh? What about sexually? How are you and Lauro? Is he satisfying you sexually?"

"That's kind of personal, Doc."

"But that's what I'm here for, to work on you personally."

She looked down again and stated, "Well, now that you mention it, no, he isn't."

"Oh, and why is that?"

"He doesn't think about what I want. He doesn't want to satisfy me; he just uses me to satisfy himself."

"So why stay with him then?"

She replied quickly, but with a dissatisfied look, "To fit in."

Hahaha. My infatuation decreased a little when she said that, but the fire in my loins did not.

"And what would satisfy you, Maddy?"

"Honestly . . ."

"Yes . . . yes . . ."

She kept looking around the room.

"I have a fantasy of being raped. Is that wrong?"

One might be surprised by this statement, but I was not.

"It's not wrong at all. You're not the first person in that chair who has said the same thing. It's important to identify your fantasies, and use them as a guiding point for what you need."

I could describe the next few sessions and what fun we were having, all the laughs, and all the stories she shared. But I'm not writing a romantic comedy. I'll just say that, as the sessions continued, the sexual tension increased exponentially. I hesitated on making a move too quickly, as I wanted to act when her interest was at its peak, otherwise I'd receive a negative response. I had to partake in the game in order to get the grand trophy. But it wasn't difficult. I myself possessed a natural charisma that made her easily captivated by me. And with each session, her body language became more enticed by me with each passing second.

Some might think it irregular that a young teenager was interested in an older male, but it wasn't at all. I had teenage patients before, and they all expressed sexual fantasies of people older than themselves. However, interest and acting on that interest were quite different. And I could tell that Maddy knew the thin line was getting blurrier with each session. I knew she thought it was wrong, and that's what made it so right. She just had to have a taste of forbidden fruit. And I had to have a taste of forbidden fruit. She just looked so delicious.

But I didn't just leave it to my mystique. The medication I prescribed her, clonazepam, also helped immensely. She was so enthralled by me that she didn't even bother to look up what I was giving her. Or maybe it was because, with the high dosage I assigned her, she suffered from drowsiness and fatigue, which impaired her decision-making ability, and enhanced my ability to dominate her. I was impressed with her resolve. The medication wasn't some sort of special drug that I concocted, nor did it make her my slave, but it did erode her will. The thought of dominating her became a daily fantasy of mine, even when I was having my fun with my secretary.

Then one day, the time came to make a move. No particular act caused this; I just noticed that the sexual tension was its peak, and it would decrease if I didn't act.

So in a session, after some banter with Maddy, I had the following exchange.

"So Maddy, we briefly discussed this before, but tell me about your rape fantasy."

"Well . . . umm . . ."

"It's okay, take your time."

"It's just . . . I'm not sure I feel comfortable talking about it."

I know you want to talk about it. Stop fighting it.

"Maddy, it's important to share these hidden feelings inside of you. If you don't let it out, it could build up and come out in terrifying ways."

Take it from me. I know that better than anyone.

184

She still just sat in silence, trying and failing to vocalize.

"Is it because I'm a man?"

She looked up, stared for a second, and then slowly nodded.

"Well then, I assure you there is nothing wrong with expressing your sexual desires to the opposite sex. Any person you express it to might even share similar desires, even your psychiatrist."

"You do?"

Much more than you know. But I'm not here to talk about me. I'm here to talk about you. But I probably spend more time focusing on myself rather than listening to other people.

"We're not here to talk about me, Maddy. We're here to talk about you. I probably listen to other people more than I actually spend time with myself."

"It's true. You are more educated and well-equipped than any person for me to tell you this."

No, you don't need an education or to be anybody special to listen to someone. I sat through ten years of classes and I don't even do it. It's kind of sad that her "loved ones" don't love her enough to listen to her feelings.

"Well, here goes. The truth is that I think Lauro is the bitch of the relationship. He doesn't really control me when we're having sex. He acts all nervous and doesn't put any power or intention behind it. I always have to initiate it. And the truth is . . . I just want to be dominated. I just want to totally lose control.

"As a woman, I feel like I have to act a certain way. I have to do this, or I have to do that. And every single day of my life is spent trying to fight that dogma . . . I learned that word from Robbie. . . . But doing that day after day is exhausting, and I just want some time where someone other than myself is controlling me, and Lauro isn't . . . no, cannot do that."

I take it back. I was fully invested in every word she was saying, but when a woman talks about sex, of course I'm going to be interested in it. Though she was barely a woman, it barely made a difference.

"Yes, yes. Thank you for telling me all this. It feels good to let this out, doesn't it?"

"Yes, yes. It feels freeing."

"But I think we can go deeper. Tell me specifically about this fantasy you have."

She illustrated, "Well, imagine this. I'm blindfolded. My arms and feet are both tied to a bed by chains. No matter how hard I try to resist them, the chains are still attached to me. But then I stop resisting and I don't feel the chains anymore, and then soon, well, you can probably guess what I start to feel next."

I got up from my desk and stood in front of Maddy. Her eyes were wide. Her pupils were dilated and her tongue was licking her lips.

"I think we can go even deeper. Close your eyes."

She slowly closed them.

"Do you feel anything different?"

"I . . . I . . ."

And then I got up close to her, I grabbed her hands, and I started kissing her neck. She started gasping, but then immediately said, "Don't stop!" And then I started kissing more and I couldn't stop, and she gasped more and more all through the hour.

And then it sort of became routine. We would do our session, and then we would have sex. She would come and then she would cum. I had sex with her on all the furniture in that office to keep it from being boring. Again, I possessed no remorse in engaging with someone so young. Age really was only a number, and she could really do it at that age.

But then, one time after we were having sex, while we put our clothes back on, she was gloomy. She put on a sad face and stood there frowning.

"Robbie . . . I mean, Robert. I have to tell you something."

Yes, we can use the desk next time.

"Robert, I don't think we can do this anymore. . . . I mean, I still want you to be my psychiatrist, but . . . I don't think we can do . . . this. It just . . . feels wrong. I have the freedom to do it, but I don't feel complete. So maybe that means there's more to this than just freedom. I just want to forget this happened and be with Lauro."

I totally understand.

"I totally understand."

"You do?"

"Yes. I was never forcing you into anything, so if you want to stop, we can stop."

"Oh thank you, Robert!"

And she hugged me, while I was still putting on my shirt, quite tightly, I might add.

"Okay, I have to go, but I'll see you soon!"

And then she left. But she would come back, and not just for the session, but for me. You see, my chains were still wrapped around her. She said that she doesn't want more now, but she won't forget the fun we had. And as soon as she's with that loser boyfriend of hers for a period of time, she'll start asking, "What if?" and long for something else. She'd long for me.

I was starting to long for her right now, and she had just barely left. But I had a solution for that. I picked up my office phone and dialed.

"Ashley, can you come in here please?"

End of Entry

18.

MIRROR IMAGE

Doctor Robert's Journal: "Robbie Shelby"

"Doctor, this is the last time, okay?" Maddy said as she was fastening her bra, and I was nibbling her neck.

"Perfectly okay." I said, as I was zipping up my pants.

As I suspected, Ms. Phrey couldn't get enough of me and kept on coming back. Her mind was telling her how wrong it was, but her body was telling her how right it was. So of course, after one of our sessions she would proclaim how finished she was with me, but at the very next session she would say she had unfinished business with me. The pattern repeated until she was out of high school and into college. Except this time, she had something else on her mind today.

"Doctor, there's someone else I want you to see. His name is Robbie. His dad passed away recently, and his mom passed away some time ago. He could really use someone to care about him, so that's why I recommended him to come and see you."

Because when you care about someone, you should immediately tell them that someone else should care about them instead.

"I'll be happy to see him, as long as he is willing to pay attention."

As long as he is willing to pay.

"Thanks, Doctor, but you see . . . "

I stared at her for a second.

"Well, you see, he's very stubborn, so I hope he's able to listen."

I smiled, on the inside and out. I touched her chin and lifted it a little so she was looking up at me.

"Don't you worry, Maddy. I know exactly how to deal with difficult patients."

Early in my career, as I mentioned, most of my patients didn't put up much of a fuss, and I was able to put them under my thumb with ease. That said, there were times I encountered difficult patients who resisted more than the others. When I encountered one, I changed tactics slightly. While I still continually reassured them of my qualifications and countered their objections, I found that it wasn't always sufficient. I had to make myself a mirror image of them. I had to make them see that they were like me, which would lower their guard.

As I grew acquainted with my patients, they'd obviously tell me about their personal lives. I would then utilize this information to foster a connection with them. If a patient enjoyed football and planned to watch a game, I made sure to watch the game myself, using moments from it as talking points for my session. If someone had a particular hobby, I would research the hobby and sometimes even participate in it to gain firsthand experiences to share. For instance, if I had a baseball player, I'd visit the batting cages; if I had a dancer, I'd take dance lessons; if I had a writer, I'd start writing my own fiction. A psychiatrist will say that their patients push them to be better people, and that was perhaps truer for my patients than any others.

What was so striking about these exercises was how much my patients resembled me, not just the difficult ones, but the regular ones as well. I consistently succeeded in cultivating a relationship, and it was because I was able to convey that I was just like them. And I was. I heard every sad story imaginable as soon as a person walked through that door. At first, it was pathetic, but then I realized as I got older, that I was pathetic. We're all just woeful souls searching for a savior to come rescue us.

But I wasn't a savior. I made them think I was their savior so I could do what I wanted, whether it was taking their money, having fun with them, or killing them. I didn't feel any remorse for what I was doing at all.

I felt empowered when I was disempowering someone.

And so I found myself on the brink of doing it once more. Eventually, Robbie reached out and scheduled a session with me. Maddy helped me prepare for it. She explained that he possessed a deep passion for art, whether it was literature, film, or the like. So I ordered a reproduction of van Gogh's *Prisoners Exercising* and put it on the back wall of my office. It was a pale imitation of the original, but it would suit my purpose. I knew he would grasp the irony, drawing him in quickly rather than repelling him. All the while, I delved into a few books in preparation for my session, so it would seem like I was interested in what he was interested in.

He finally came in.

"Please, take a seat."

And he did, without saying anything. I could tell he was thoroughly vexed, as he kept squirming around in the chair, taking in the surroundings with an annoyed smirk on his face.

I chose to read a book because he read them as well, and it would immediately catch his interest to find a point of commonality between us.

As he settled into his seat, I pretended I was reading, not giving him the time of day. My aim was to subtly assert my power over him. According to Maddy, he was a man who didn't respect authority, thus a traditional approach wouldn't interest him. I couldn't ask him how his day was, or why he was here; I wouldn't get a good response. But by acting disinterested, it inadvertently communicated a lack of respect, a behavior that he respected, if not immediately. This strategy would eventually compel him to do the talking, driving him to a point of rage.

Suddenly, after a few minutes, "You know, for a psychiatrist you're not doing a great job. I thought you're supposed to show some care and concern for your patients, not bury yourself in a book like you encountered your first porn magazine."

Told you. He threw out more insults, some of them good, and I laughed, until I finally said, "I have a name."

"What?"

"I have a name. My name is Doctor Robert Wolfe, but you can call me Doctor Robert. Can you do that?

"What??"

"Can you say the following phrase: 'Hello, Doctor Robert'?"

Begrudgingly, he did as asked. "Hel-lo, Doc-tor Rob-ert."

And our relationship blossomed from there. I admit, he was probably the toughest patient I ever had in getting him to trust me. But like all my patients, he eventually acceded.

We then had a routine. I would have a book that I was reading. We would talk about it. And then I would weave the discussion back into his life. He would raise a point and then I would raise a counterpoint. Like anyone else, he frequently rocked back and forth between trusting me and not trusting me. But as I said, he rocked longer than any other patient I've had before. It was a long con, but as soon as he entered that door, he was mine.

And when he did finally buy into what I was saying, he almost seemed happier. Almost. By acting like everyone else, he still was just another woeful soul looking for a savior.

And that's why I will kill him. Partly because he didn't belong here, and hasn't figured out how to. But mostly because I wanted to empower myself. I haven't figured out how yet, but I will.

I said to him once, 'Remember, Robbie, all people are equal.' But I left out an important part. All people are equal. But some people are more equal than others.

End of Entry

PART 4:
WATERLOO SUNSET

19.

PENULTIMATE

My brain lurched. My mouth fell silent. The information refused to settle in my mind, despite it being the third time I had read it.

Lauro, that poor dumb fool who did the doctor's dirty work. Maddy, who was sexually abused by the doctor, and disturbingly found pleasure in it. All the other people who weren't even mentioned. Entries I skipped past because it was just too painful to read. It occurred to me that it didn't read like a traditional journal. It seemed so implausible that journal entries could be this comprehensive, but that's how I knew it was real. It was so detailed and revealing that someone with knowledge of each individual had to have written it.

It was unfathomable that someone so sadistic was walking on this earth. A human so lacking in humanity that he didn't care who he hurt. And that's why I had to do something. Or at least that's what I kept telling myself.

I put down the manuscript at a booth in Joe Schmoe's. The bar was its usual self, a constant in a world of uncertainties. Doubtless I needed to describe something that never changed. I craved a change of scenery, having spent countless days cooped up in my apartment, lost in thought. Maybe I should have been concerned about carrying Doctor Robert's manuscript with me. But then I realized no one would give a damn that I had a written manuscript with me. Nobody had cared that I was underage and had been going to this bar many times over.

I was at a loss for what to do. I tried texting and calling Maddy and Lauro to discuss what I had just read. The journals revealed deep struggles they were facing—struggles I was too ignorant and self-absorbed to see, so I desired to talk with them about their struggles. But they weren't responding. Maybe I was at the bar to see if some shining light would drop down on me. Maybe some unseen person would swoop in and save me.

But none of those fanciful ideas played out that night. I was, as I always have been, alone. If this was to the contrary, I wouldn't be here right now. It actually came to the point where I tried to imagine people in the seat in front of me, and what they might say. I tried to imagine Rebecca in her leather jacket, and what witty joke she might make. I tried to imagine Vinnie, and whether he would seethe in rage at the revelation of Doctor Robert's true nature. I tried to imagine Rachel, and whether she could help me forget about yesterday. I tried to imagine my dad, to see if he could encourage me in this trying time. I even tried to imagine my mom, and see if she had any words of wisdom for me. But no matter how many times I tried, my imagination always faded into an empty seat in front of me.

I was stuck with my own powers. So I might as well think through it, and not get caught up in indecision. If I did nothing, and carried on with my life, eventually Doctor Robert would notice his manuscript was gone, and I would be the prime suspect. He already wanted to kill me. True, I was no longer his patient and was aware of who he really was, but it hardly mattered. His twisted nature would likely drive him to murder me regardless. And besides that, I couldn't just let him get away with this. But if I was going to do something, what would I do? I couldn't kill Doctor Robert. I'm no murderer. I lacked the power to do it. So the option I was really left with was to bring this to the police. However, I couldn't simply hand it over. I did just commit a crime to acquire it. And it would be stolen evidence, which was inadmissible in court. So no option was perfect.

I could just walk away. I could leave the city, and let someone else solve the problem. But what kind of person would I be to do that? Did I really lack the strength to stand up to injustice? Would anyone else?

CHAPTER 19: PENULTIMATE

As I pondered this, I observed the faces around me. And each face proved to be dejected, or with a fake smile. I used to believe that my sleepless nights were my burden alone. But Maddy and Lauro turned out to be just as troubled as I was. Doctor Robert was almost a reflection of myself. In another life, I could have let the power get to my head and destroy everything around me. And these poor souls in the bar probably each had their own sob story or a tale of woe. In truth, I bet every single soul has stayed awake into the wee hours of the night.

WATERLOO SUNSET

I stared at my Waterloo Sunset, wondering what to do. I always looked at it for answers, because I couldn't come up with them on my own. I kept on looking for as long as I could. But the longer I looked, the harder it was to turn away. So I finally did turn away. I realized at that moment, my Waterloo Sunset wasn't empowering me. It was a distraction. It proved a helpful outlet, but I relied on it too much. I looked at that sunset more times than I could count. And all of those times, I could have been doing something else. I could have been working. I could have been trying to find friends. I could have been trying to stop Doctor Robert earlier. But I was so preoccupied by what I could be doing that I never did anything. So I finally gathered the power to turn away.

After thinking long into the night, I realized that there was only one thing I could do. I had to stop Doctor Robert.

• • •

"Doctor Robert?" I asked as I entered his pitch-black office. I sped past his secretary and barged through the door with intention.

"Robbie? I thought you wanted nothing to do with me."

"I have something to say that you might want to hear."

"Come in then."

Doctor Robert wasn't reading anything this time. But he was playing with his laptop on his desk. I quickly sat down, eager to rub what I had done in his face.

"So Robbie, how are you feeling?"

I sat in silence for a long time.

"Robbie?"

"You know, Doctor, I think that's the first time you asked me that. But I know now, you don't care how I am feeling."

"What?"

"You can drop the act, Doctor. I know what you did."

He kept looking perplexed as I kept talking.

"I know everything."

He simply gazed at me, speechless. His little house of cards started to tumble. And then the door slammed open behind me in a matter of seconds. A detective, clad in a suit, burst in, swiftly drawing his gun and aiming it at the doctor.

I was shocked, but then I understood that after I planted that journal at a police station, they must have identified me and followed me, so they could locate Robert. I knew I would be incriminated if I told the police I took the journal from his house, so I had to be more indirect about it. I wrapped up that journal in a package and addressed it to my local police station. I knew if I entered the station with that kind of package, I wouldn't be able to leave. So I scouted out the station for a few days, waiting for an opening. Once again, I wore a hood and sunglasses to cover my identity. Finally, a delivery driver parked outside the station in a van. The woman got out of the van, opened the back of it, grabbed some boxes, and left the back open, suggesting that she would return. I discreetly walked over and placed the package in the delivery driver's van from the back, knowing the driver would likely deliver it to the police. And I wanted to talk with Robert one last time before he faced the music. I was confident that he wouldn't have tried anything to me. And even if he did, it wouldn't have mattered. I was surprised the police acted so quickly and decided to arrest him while I was in a session. But the momentary shock faded, and turned to happiness.

"Doctor, you aren't going to hurt anyone anymore. I read your journal and I know everything you did. You have no power over me anymore."

I turned to the detective, "Arrest the criminal."

The doctor continued to stare, but then he smiled, and started to laugh.

"You heard him."

The detective then pointed the gun straight at my face. Doctor Robert turned his laptop around, revealing security footage of me breaking into his house.

"You're clever, Robbie. But not clever enough. I knew you were going to try something like this. Lauro and Maddy told me you were going to subvert me somehow, and the only plausible explanation was that you intended to steal from me. And I goaded you into trying to steal from my house, since I offered for you to come there. I commend your caution in how you planted my 'journal,' and it was smart to attempt to conceal your identity while breaking into my house. But once I presented this footage to the police, it was over for you.

"You can try and say that it wasn't you who stole from me, but you just admitted to the crime in front of the officer. The figure in this footage looks similar in build to you, and I'm sure forensic evidence and your DNA can be found in the journal. No one else would have the motive to steal anything besides this journal from my house. No one else could have stolen this from my home besides you. Now, breaking and entering is a misdemeanor, but coupled with theft is home invasion, which is a felony. That comes with years in prison, the maximum being life imprisonment."

Okay . . . for just stealing a journal, it's unlikely I'd receive life imprisonment. Maybe I'd receive a few years in prison, which would be difficult, but not impossible.

"But you didn't just try to hurt me, did you, Robbie? You also hurt your friends."

"That's not true." I said.

"Maddy came to me and said you sexually assaulted her. You physically assaulted Lauro. Both of them will testify that you tied both of them up against their will, and made them watch while you enacted your desires."

Stunned, my mouth was held wide open in shock. "That's not true." I said again.

"Both Maddy and Lauro possess bruises and signs of attack." The detective placed photos on the table. Maddy and Lauro wore torn-up shirts and bedraggled pants. Lauro had bruises on his face and body, while Maddy had a black eye. I couldn't believe what I saw in front of me. Any strength I had was quickly zapped from my body. The chill down my spine was so cold that I couldn't move at all. Where was that? Who could have done that?

"You did that, Robbie. Maddy has explained in our sessions that you've always been fond of her, and that you tried to come on to her many times. She always resisted, but you always persisted. Which makes sense—you never really saw them as your friends. You only saw them as lesser-thans.

"So, if you couple home invasion, assault, sexual assault, and a whole long list of other crimes you just committed, you're looking at a long prison sentence, Robbie. It's unlikely you'll see the light of day. I'm afraid, our sessions must conclude here. It's been a pleasure while it lasted, and I hope I've empowered you somewhat. I think you're going to need it."

The detective grabbed me, put my hands behind my back, and handcuffed me. As he was pushing me out, I blurted out, "Wait! Didn't you read that journal? This man is no doctor. He's committed crimes too numerous to name. If I am going to be held accountable for my supposed actions, then I want this man to be held accountable for his."

"Robbie, at best it would be stolen evidence, which is inadmissible in court. But it doesn't matter, Robbie. I wrote that journal the night before you broke into my house. As I said, I knew you were going to rob me, so I planted bait for you. All of that journal is just nonsense that I wrote as it came out of my head. Do you really believe that I would be that dejected to leave a confession of all my supposed crimes lying around my house?"

He smiled, but I could see right through that smile.

"He's lying. Don't believe him!"

But the detective just shook his head in disapproval and shoved me through the door. As I was being led through the halls, I was so demoralized and disempowered that I began to cry, wondering what left of my life there was.

• • •

I stormed through my apartment door. I just wanted someone to talk to. I called Lauro and there was no answer. I called Maddy, and it rang a few times but then went to voicemail. I called again, and it rang even less, and still went to voicemail. I texted Maddy and Lauro, begging for them to talk to me, but I still received no response for the rest of the night.

I pondered the reasons why Lauro and Maddy refused to communicate with me. And I eventually visualized Maddy in my room, as if she were next to me. She scolded me and said, "Robbie, were we ever really friends? All you ever did was mock us and barely even noticed us when we were together. No matter how many times we tried to integrate you in our lives, you always resisted. You never took any interest in me and Lauro's life. It wasn't true friendship, Robbie. You started to change, but then you changed for the worse. You decided to go after Doctor Robert, one of the few people who empowered me in my life. So we did what we could so you can never hurt him again. We can't take care of you anymore, Robbie. But maybe this is what you want too, because you always disliked being around us, so you don't have to be around us anymore."

Or at least, that's what I thought she would say. I tried to imagine the conversation in a few different ways, but each time left me sadder than the last. So I stopped and tried to look at my situation.

I was able to pay for bail, but the astronomical cost took the rest of my savings and the college fund my parents had for me. As Robert said, I was being charged with a long list of crimes, a likelihood of life imprisonment. I could try and fight the charges, but how could I? Doctor Robert had me dead to rights with his footage, and as he explained, no one else would just steal a journal from a man's home. And in my anger, I had admitted to the crime. As for Maddy and Lauro's testimony, it wouldn't just be their words against mine. It appears that they colluded with Doctor Robert to fabricate evidence of wrongdoing to place me in prison. And unfortunately, I couldn't hire a lawyer, as I had no money left, and I doubted an appointed attorney would be able to pull any strings. Maybe if I plea-bargained I could get a minimum sentence, and then restart my life after that. But how hard would it be to find a job with a criminal record? And even if I could, would life even be worth living with that sort of stain? But maybe since it would be my first offense, I would receive a reduced punishment.

But even as I pondered that route further, I realized that I likely wouldn't get the minimum sentence. I thought further about the exchange with Doctor Robert and the detective. I noticed how Doctor Robert had his laptop on his desk, immediately ready to present the footage, as if he was tipped off. I noticed how quickly the detective appeared as soon as I walked into Doctor Robert's office. I noticed how the detective placed the photos on the table, seemingly showing off for no reason. I noticed Maddy and Lauro's injuries in the photos, again implying the injuries and any other sort of evidence was falsified. And I noticed how Doctor Robert almost seemingly ordered the detective around, as if the detective was his underling.

I didn't know how, but it looked like Doctor Robert was embedded with the police. It was hard for me to understand why the police would protect him. But maybe it was less about protection and more about business, as I'm sure he had money to spare. But since he possessed connections with the law, a lenient prison sentence seemed unlikely. And even if I did get a lesser sentence, with the types of connections Robert had, would something even more horrible happen to me? Would I face an unfortunate accident in prison? Would I be killed as soon as I walked inside the prison building? My mind staggered at the possibilities, each one even more disempowering than the last. I had no one to talk to about it.

There was only one thing I could think of. I went into my closet. I reached for the highest shelf, grabbed the shoebox, and put it on my bed. I opened it and removed the double-action revolver from within.

I went outside my veranda and took a seat on the balcony railing, my feet dangling over the building. My Waterloo Sunset was fading from existence, almost like my life. And I felt so powerless that the sunset couldn't fill the void in my aching heart any longer.

Even after everything, I was still staring at this sunset. But now I had no choice. I would be in a prison cell soon, forced to survive without such a view. And Doctor Robert would get away scot-free. It was funny how one little mistake could cost you your life. But I didn't have a life anymore. I don't think I ever had a life. Even with everything stacked against me, I wasn't a true fighter. My life had just been one roller coaster of tragedy, and it wasn't going to stop. Look at what I'd lost. My mom, my dad, Rachel, Rebecca, Vinnie, and now Maddy and Lauro. I had nothing left.

When the light had almost faded, I looked at the sunset one last time. I felt none of its potency. My life was at an end. And I lacked any power to change it.

EPILOGUE

THE WOLF DEN

In the wee hours of the night, three men sat at a dinner table in a luxurious restaurant, feasting on a mighty meal. The table was filled with succulent and flavorful food, especially all kinds of meat—pork, steak, and lamb. One of these men was Doctor Robert, in a three-piece-suit.

"Gentlemen, I would like to thank you again for your continued support in my . . . business affairs. And as a token of goodwill, please accept these gifts to continue doing business."

Doctor Robert handed the two gentlemen envelopes. They opened them, noted that they were filled with cash, and closed them. Who these two men were didn't matter, as they didn't matter to Doctor Robert. Meetings like this became routine, and the faces were interchangeable to him.

"You are too kind."

"Oh, save it, I know you will gladly take my money any day. But as long as this keeps you out of my affairs, it is worth the price."

One of the men jumped in, "You know Doctor, it would be way less expensive for you if you decided not to pursue your 'affairs' the way you do. Why do you do this? Why can't you help people like any other doctor?"

The two men both stared at the doctor, eagerly waiting for an answer.

"If I answered that question simply, I have a feeling you two would leave here unsatisfied. So if you will indulge me, I will be happy to answer that question with a story.

"There was once this farm that was run by animals. The farm was filled with all types of animals—ducks, cows, horses, pigs, and much more. These animals had more intellectuality than other animals, but they were still fundamentally animals. However, due to their increased intellectual capacity, after many years they were able to make advances in technology to make their lives easier. They even developed laws that told all the animals how to act. Even with some ups and downs, the farm and its society they created succeeded, at least for a time.

"Before these advancements, the animals all had to work day in and day out, with little time for themselves. As time went on, the animals didn't get used to all this freedom they had, as the technology was doing the work for them. This resulted in them being depressed all the time, as they had more time to be alone, and they were scared when they were alone. A cow would aimlessly wander the farm, feeling lost and purposeless without any work. Or a duck would spend long hours alone in a pond, isolated and longing for any social interaction.

"To compensate, the animals started to spend time with each other. But this inevitably caused problems. Opposing animals didn't know how to interact with each other. Ducks were unable to interact with horses. Cows were unable to interact with sheep. Ducks couldn't understand a horse's preference for running, nor could a horse understand a duck's preference for swimming. Cows couldn't understand a sheep's preference for whistling, and sheep couldn't understand a cow's preference for grunting. So much diversity existed on the farm that the animals focused more on what made them different than alike.

"So rather than the animals trying to respect these differences, they all decided they would interact with each other in a very specific way, using social cues. The animals didn't desire to understand the other animals or how they interacted. So they created social cues so they didn't have to understand. They didn't value difference, so they created these cues so everyone could be the same. The problem was, there was no rulebook on how to utilize them. No one knew how to define it or impose it, due to so much variation. This would inevitably lead to misunderstandings when interacting with each other, causing more depression within the farm. The animals would frequently host workshops or community events to bridge these gaps. All the animals would attend them, but none of the animals would learn anything from it. They went through the motions of acknowledging difference, without truly valuing or understanding it. They put little effort into learning the differences, and even less effort into actually interacting with others.

"But the animal that didn't fit in the most was the wolf. It was difficult for the wolf to reconcile his predatory instincts, but through self-discipline he managed to put others before himself. Due to the advancements in technology, the wolf was able to survive without eating other members of the farm. Each animal received rations to live, and for the carnivores like the wolf, the rations were synthetic but could still sate them. Many animals would protest the amount of rations they received, but only the wolf refused to protest. When he got hungry, he refrained from stealing other rations, or eating other animals. An occasional thought would drift through his mind, but he could always restrain himself. The wolf faced more challenges than any other animal, but the increased adversity increased the wolf's power.

"But even so, the rest of the animals were still afraid of the wolf. He originally wasn't from the farm. No one knew where he came from, where he was going, or what he wanted in life, which made him more terrifying. Every time the wolf would approach a sheep, the sheep would always run away. The sheep would explain that the wolf's approach was wrong, and no matter what approach the wolf took, it was always wrong. Every time the wolf spoke, all the animals ignored what he said, and all the animals noticed his foreboding fangs. They all noticed what made the wolf different, rather than the same. They all took one look at the wolf and thought he would end up eating them. They could never imagine a wolf that could fit in at their farm. As such, the animals banished him from the farm because they were too scared and uncomfortable with him around.

"Outside of the farm, the wolf was able to survive, even with no support from the farm. The wolf was able to build his own little farm with no other animals. But some of the animals occasionally went to his farm to harass and deride him. Since he didn't fit in at their farm, that made it okay to mock his farm. The wolf would groan and shrug off their vexations most of the time. However, the more maltreatment the wolf received, the more the beast inside him grew. And the maltreatment would sometimes be so extreme that the wolf would have to flash his teeth and drive them from his farm. The animals would go back to their farm, proclaiming how scary the wolf was and demanding the wolf be killed. All the farm animals eventually agreed, and in the night, while the wolf was sleeping, they set fire to his farm, thinking they killed him.

"But they didn't kill the wolf. He smelled the fire before it reached him and ran away from the farm as it burned from afar. As the wolf looked over his smoldering home, he realized that if he would forever be known only as a wolf, then he would be the wolf, only not the one they imagined.

"The wolf knew the only way to survive was to get back into the farm. And if the wolf couldn't be a wolf, then he had to be someone else. Soon, the wolf spied on the farm animals, specifically the sheep. The sheep provided support for all the farm. They contributed clothing and consoled the other animals while they worked. Many sheep were some of the most well-off animals on the farm because there were so many animals that needed comfort, and they were appropriately compensated for it. The animals could not find support among themselves, as they didn't know how to interact with each other, and interactions that they didn't understand made them uncomfortable. So the animals all relied on the sheep for guidance and comfort since they could not find it among others.

"One day, the wolf snuck up on an unsuspecting sheep and killed him. The wolf tore off all of the sheep's clothing and put it on himself. The wolf examined the sheep's behavior so closely that he learned how to act like a sheep, though in truth he injected much behavior from being the wolf into his persona. He was more of a wolf than a sheep, but was never suspected because he was the savior of the farm, and a savior can do no wrong.

"Some time afterwards, the wolf began to eat lambs from the farm out of spite. Many of the lambs didn't harm the wolf, but he knew they would if they knew his true nature. The more the wolf ate, the more the wolf grew a taste for it. The wolf knew that he couldn't attempt to eat all the animals, because he would be caught. He knew that he had to focus exclusively on the lambs if he wanted to feed the beast inside him. The lambs were the easiest target because they were the weakest of the animals. Occasionally, when no one was looking, he would eat larger animals, like a horse or a cow. But he always had to restrain himself, lest his true nature was caught by the farm.

"As time passed and the wolf grew old, he eventually passed away and the sheep's clothing was removed from his body. And the farm animals were in disbelief. They could not believe someone who could help people was also someone who could hurt people. So they just denied it and carried on with their lives.

"Soon after, more wolves began to assimilate themselves, crippling the farm. Whether this was due to other wolves observing how he performed, or them finding out themselves, who's to say? But wolves were injecting themselves into the farm. And the animals still refused to comprehend that a wolf could be a sheep. So the wolves ate all the animals until there were no animals left. And the farm was no longer an animal farm, but a wolf den."

Doctor Robert finished speaking, and began to finish his meal, which was mostly lamb.

One of the men interjected, "I think I understand."

The other replied, "I know I do, but you realize that we can't protect you forever; sooner or later, you will be caught."

"There might be a day where the world realizes who I am. But that day hasn't come yet."

As he spoke, Doctor Robert finished his mighty lamb. But Doctor Robert was still hungry.

ABOUT THE AUTHOR

Bobby Lopez is an old soul who rocks and rolls.
He reads and writes through the nights.
And can rhyme, time after time.